CARAMEL CORRUPTION

BOOK SIX IN THE CUPCAKE CRIMES SERIES

MOLLY MAPLE

MARY E. TWOMEY, LLC

CARAMEL CORRUPTION

Book Six in the Cupcake Crimes Series

By

Molly Maple

COPYRIGHT

To my son Kroi,

May we get through your teen years with kindness, cuddles and cupcakes.

ABOUT CARAMEL CORRUPTION

**When the past comes back to haunt Marianne,
Charlotte knows she must take action.**

When Marianne's ex-fiancé shows up with a problem he
cannot solve without her help, Charlotte McKay makes it
her business to stick close to Marianne's side.

With a body in his trunk and a track record of skirting the
truth, the case against Jeremy is looking to be open and
shut. But when the facts don't add up, Charlotte is sure
that the only crime Jeremy is guilty of is breaking
Marianne's heart. Charlotte knows she must prove
Jeremy's innocence before it's too late.

"Caramel Corruption" is filled with layered clues and cozy

moments, written by Molly Maple, which is a pen name for a USA Today bestselling author.

GOOD FRIEND, OLD FLAME

I was stifling my groans an hour ago when we were moving the furniture into Carlos' new office, but after unloading the millionth box of legal briefs from the moving truck, I don't hold back. "Ugh. I think I pulled a muscle."

Marianne's brows pinch together. "Which one?"

"All of them."

Marianne snickers as she sets down a large box beside mine on the long, oval table. The walls are a boring white and the floor is a honey-colored wood. I sure hope one of these boxes has decorations in them.

Marianne swipes the sweat off her brow as she grins up at me. "Have I mentioned how grateful I am that you're helping me move Carlos into his new office?"

"You did. Have I mentioned how happy I am that your boyfriend doesn't live two hours away anymore?"

Marianne is still new to the idea of referring to the big city lawyer as her boyfriend. Her neck shrinks as the tips of her ears turn pink. "Telling me his boss is putting him in charge of opening a new branch in Hamshire was quite the conversation. I timed the drive from my house to his office. Twenty-two minutes, Charlotte. We'll only be twenty-two minutes away from each other."

Carlos is still outside, but I lower my voice all the same. "You sure it's okay with you? You would tell him if it was moving too fast, right?"

Marianne starts stacking the boxes to make room for more. "We've been dating, doing the phone thing for a few months now. It's a big step, but I like it." She smiles, her short brown hair swishing across her chin. "I like him. Doesn't make me guess as to what he's thinking. Doesn't make me worry he's cheating." Her expression tightens, so I know she is thinking about Jeremy—the man she was with for years, who ended their engagement by cheating on her. "Carlos is a good man. He treats me like I'm special."

"That's because you are special." Before I can keep my true feelings inside, a shadow crosses over my mood. "Have I told you lately how much I loathe your ex-fiancé? I never met the guy, but to have put you through a long-distance relationship while he was cheating on you... I'm glad Carlos is a solid guy."

"Me, too. Living only twenty-two minutes away from

him will be nice. The drive was a real drain." Her eyebrows dance. "Now we can double date more often."

"I like the sound of that. What's the next town event?" My mouth pulls to the side while I stretch my arms over my head. "Or does Sweetwater Falls take a break from town festivals during the winter months?"

Marianne chuckles as Carlos comes in with another giant box of... I'm guessing important lawyerly things. "Oh, no. We just move the events indoors. In a couple of weeks, there's the Knit Your Heart Out fair."

Carlos tilts his head to the side, wiping his forehead with the back of his hand. Though he usually wears a crisp suit or nice business casual clothing, today this man in his forties is in jeans and a polo, with a winter hat covering his dark hair. Even after spending all morning lifting heavy things, his posture is still perfect. "Knit Your Heart Out? That sounds like it would only happen in Sweetwater Falls," Carlos comments with a winded smile. "I'm in."

I love the sound of everything in Sweetwater Falls. Back when I lived in a big city, if I had heard of an event with that title, I wouldn't think twice, but in the sweet small town I adore, suddenly I can't think of anything cuter than a fair to celebrate knitting. "Let's get tickets to that, for sure. Is it like, people knit blankets and sell them for charity?"

Marianne giggles at what I thought was a solid guess. "Ho, no. I mean, sure, there are blankets. But it's so much more fun than that. The local book club, As the Page Turns, puts on the fair every January to raise money for their book club. They knit all sorts of crazy things. It's a blast. No matter how many items are for sale, they sell out every year."

I rack my brain for different things a person could knit. "Blankets, winter hats, mittens. What else?"

Marianne plops down on one of the chairs. Her arms flop over the arms of the seat, her legs sprawled because it's been that long of a day. "Stuffed animals, of course. Sweaters. They knit potholders, ties, tea cozies, slippers, socks with funny sayings on them. Then there's a whole section of cross-stitch stuff. One year, they auctioned off a cross-stitch piece that was a picture of Rip, the Town Selectman, sitting on the toilet. Sold for two hundred dollars. I'm still mad I got outbid."

My eyes bug. "Whoa! That's pretty cool. I didn't realize you could do so much with yarn. The Live Forever Club has been knitting more than usual this week. I should pay closer attention to what they're making." I roll my eyes at myself. "I am useless with knitting needles."

Marianne grins at me. "Don't let Agnes hear you say that. She'll make it her mission to educate you."

Carlos picks up Marianne's arm and massages her wrist. His skin is a few shakes darker than her olive hue. They are so cute together. "I love that it won't be a two-hour drive to go to the town events anymore. I have never been more excited to go to a knitting fair."

Marianne's eyes close at the pampering. "I'm so glad you're moving to Hamshire. That's so close."

Carlos jerks his thumb to the front door of the office. "My stuff is moved into my condo. That's the last of the boxes for the office. The sign is hanging outside. Now it's just a matter of unpacking and setting things up. Then I'm officially here."

"I love it." Marianne might start drooling if Carlos keeps massaging her wrist. "I am never leaving this conference room. Too tired."

When the front door of the office opens, the three of us blink at each other in confusion. "Is that your boyfriend, Charlotte?" Carlos asks me.

It's so strange that that is a legitimate question. I'm not used to being a girl who has a boyfriend. If it was anyone else, I might feel strange about it all, but as it's Logan, a smile toys with my lips whenever the topic of our relationship comes up.

I shake my head in Carlos' direction. "Logan is ice fishing with his dad this weekend." I motion to the spot where Carlos is joined to Marianne's wrist. "Keep up the good work. I'll play the role of receptionist."

I meander into the hallway, making my way to the receptionist's desk. The smooth surface has a computer that is not hooked up yet. There is a box of office supplies on the floor next to the chair.

I smile at the man standing in front of the desk. He is wearing cowboy boots that look new, paired with clean jeans and a pressed dress shirt tucked in. He is lean with long arms and legs, and looks like he's only ever worn cowboy western clothing for the fashion, and not for any actual ranch work.

I flash a breezy smile at the newcomer. "Hi, there. Welcome to Bankman and Voss. What can I help you with today?"

I am sweaty, despite the winter weather outside. My blonde curls have been slapped into a messy ponytail. My knitted lavender cardigan and jeans make me look less than professional, but my tone says that I am cool, calm and in control of this new office.

The man reaches out his hand to shake mine, cluing me in to the fact that he has clammy palms. Upon further inspection, he has a line of moisture dotting his forehead and cleanshaven upper lip. "I think I'm in need of some legal assistance." He motions to the nearly empty desk. "Are you folks open for business?"

He looks to be around my age and about the same height as my five-foot-ten-inches. "We're just getting this office set up, but there is a lawyer here who can take down your information, if you like."

The man nods eagerly, his coifed blond hair rustling with the motion. It is then that I notice a hint of panic wafting off him. "Yes, please. The sooner the better." He gestures with his hand for me to speed up. "Like, right now."

My eyes widen at his urgency, but I nod politely in response. "Yes, sir. Mister…"

"Mister Johnson."

"Just one moment, Mister Johnson."

I move back down the hallway, knocking once on the conference room door just in case the two lovebirds are mid-smooch.

I poke my head inside. "Carlos, you have your first client in the foyer."

Carlos grins. "I guess this was a hot spot to set up shop. Remind me to gloat to my boss that I was right."

Marianne stands to organize the boxes atop the table. "After your meeting with your first client, I vote we go out for lunch. I'm starved."

"Done. I need to get to know the restaurants around here. My boss is paying for lunch today, so pick somewhere nice."

I feather my fingers together. "Sushi with a side of sushi with sushi on top."

Carlos chuckles as he digs a legal pad out of one of the boxes. "Deal."

Marianne's nose scrunches. "I've never tried sushi before." Then a gleam takes over her insecurity that the Live Forever Club would deem as a Marianne the Wild sort of expression. "Let's do it!"

Carlos gives us a thumbs up before he exits, but after he's gone only a few seconds, I realize Carlos isn't fully prepared to greet a new client. "He doesn't have a pen," I tell Marianne, searching through the boxes for a writing instrument.

Marianne tugs a pencil out of her pocket. "I mean, I'm the Head Librarian. I think it's part of the uniform that I have a pencil on me at all times." She smirks at me and exits the room while I set my sights on at least getting the coffee cart set up in the conference room.

I don't get more than the coffeemaker out before I hear Marianne's voice turn shrill. "What are you doing here?"

Whether or not the situation warrants rushing, I dash out in the hallway toward Marianne. Anything that causes her the least bit of distress needs to be dealt with immediately.

As her best friend, that is my duty.

When I skid into the foyer, I don't see anything obviously alarming. Mister Johnson's eyes are wide, but he is a respectable conversational distance away from Carlos and Marianne. "Oh! Hi, Marianne. I didn't realize you... Do you work here? I assumed you were still at the library, shelving books."

I don't like the way he says, "shelving books." He might as well have said, "shoveling trash."

Marianne is mute, gaping at him with confusion radiating out from her. Her eyes are wide, and her body language is taut with a fight-or-flight debate plain on her features.

Carlos motions between the two of them. "Do you two know each other?"

Marianne mouths a reply, but her volume has deserted her.

Mister Johnson supplies the answer that sends my heart plummeting. "We used to date." He shoves his hands in his pockets. "Actually, we used to be engaged."

My mouth hangs open. I am at a loss for words, which is just as well. Of all the things I have in me to say right now, most of them are unsavory swears. I have half a mind to march him straight out of here without further explanation.

Jeremy Johnson—A.K.A. the worst man in the world—has the gall to cast Marianne a sheepish smile. "Good to see you, sugarbean."

I am torn between vomiting at the stupid nickname and punching his lights out for invoking it after cheating on her like the slimeball he is.

Who on earth could possibly have the corroded soul to cheat on Marianne and break her heart? She is the most wonderful person in the world. She dreams in classic literature and always has time to help her neighbor.

Whatever led Jeremy to set foot in this law office, I am ready to ignore his issue and thrust him out the front door.

Carlos postures. "Marianne, why don't you go to the conference room and take a load off."

Marianne doesn't need more of an invitation to exit

than that. She disappears around the corner while I stand still, unable to move, lest I deck this man where he stands.

Carlos is ever the professional, though I can tell from his taut body language that he very much does not want this man in his office. "Tell me how the firm can help you, Mister Johnson."

I note clearly that Carlos said the firm can help Jeremy, and not that Carlos himself will be any part of helping his girlfriend's ex out of whatever jam he has created for himself with his shriveled heart and non-existent conscience.

Jeremy is still sweating as he jerks his chin toward the door. "It's better that I show you."

Carlos and I follow Jeremy out into the January air, shivering without our coats as we walk through the inch of unshoveled snow towards a newer black sedan.

It's a stupid car. For no reason other than that Jeremy drives it, I hate it and immediately deem it as pretentious.

Jeremy stands at the trunk, spreading his fingers out over the surface. "I'm a singer, see, on the American Pumpernickel tour. After the concert last night, I passed out in the tour bus. Usually, my manager comes and wakes me up."

Because you're a child who can't take care of himself, I say to myself in a cruel manner.

I am never this mean, but this guy broke my best friend's heart. Therefore, he will forever be scum.

His cowboy boots are ridiculous. They have never been worn for actual ranching work, I'll bet.

Jeremy touches the top of the trunk over and over while he speaks. "When I woke up and saw my manager's car parked outside the tour bus, I went over there and found him like this." Jeremy opens the backdoor, revealing a gruesome sight I am unprepared to see.

A portly man in his sixties is curled up across the backseat, his eyes open and his full lips parted. He has bruising around his neck and his hands are bound in front with a zip tie. He is balding on top, with curly brown whisps of hair encircling his head like the halo I hope he has in his afterlife.

I shriek, covering my nose to smother the smell of death. "What is... Who is... Why did you... Is he really..."

None of my half-sentences make a lick of sense, so Carlos takes the wheel. "Did you call the police?"

Jeremy tilts his hand from side to side. "Sort of. I have an old friend who I think is still a cop. I was going to take the body to him, because he'll hear me out that I had nothing to do with this. I left a message for him, then stopped here on the way to see him."

Carlos' words come out slowly. "Why would someone assume you are guilty of murder? Finding a body in a car that isn't yours isn't exactly a smoking gun."

Jeremy grimaces. "People might think it's me who did this, because my manager and I had a pretty public fight."

Carlos sighs. "That's hardly a reason not to call the police first thing."

Jeremy shoves his hands in his pockets. "I'm on my way to my buddy Logan, who is a cop in Sweetwater Falls. I saw your sign, so I stopped here. I figure I might need representation. Sweetwater Falls doesn't have a law office." Jeremy casts Carlos a sheepish expression that I want to slap off his face. "Was that wrong?"

Carlos tugs out his phone. "Police first, representation if you need it *after* the police do their thing." He puts in a call to the Hamshire police, a hard look on his face.

My fingers are clumsy as I snap a picture on my phone and send it to the sheriff of Sweetwater Falls. I also send the picture to my boyfriend, Logan Flowers, who just so happens to be Jeremy's cop buddy.

I frown as I examine the body, my eyes drawn to the man's lips. "Is there something in his mouth?" I lean in to get a closer look, pointing at something white between the man's teeth. "What is that?"

Jeremy squints. "I don't know. I didn't notice it when I moved him."

Carlos' eyes close. "You moved the body?"

Jeremy grimaces. His neck shrinks as he offers up a guilty smile, like a boy who took a cookie from the cookie jar five minutes before dinner time. "Was that bad? He was in the driver's seat. I had to move him to drive the body here."

When Jeremy reaches out his hand toward the white

something stuck in the man's mouth, Carlos' voice turns sharp. "Don't touch anything. Leave it all for the police."

Carlos talks into his phone while Jeremy stands near the car with a hapless look on his face.

If Jeremy is back until they get to the bottom of who did this, then I want to solve this murder as quick as possible, so I can get Jeremy out of Sweetwater Falls and out of Marianne's life.

2

QUESTIONS AND CLUES

*M*arianne wrings her hands as she paces across the floor of the industrial kitchen. "Is it wrong that I want to hide out here until the end of time?"

I shake my head as I put the last of the cupcakes in the walk-in refrigerator. "Not at all. You're welcome to stay here as long as you like. You've got a key. My business is your secret hideaway."

Marianne nods, not looking the least bit relieved. "I can't believe Jeremy is back in Sweetwater Falls."

"That's the part you can't believe? I can't believe your ex showed up with a body in the backseat. I also can't believe that Logan and the sheriff still have their phones turned off. I'm not the kind of person to begrudge anyone a little quality father-son time on their ice fishing trip, but

I'll feel better when they are home and on the case. I've never been to Apple Blossom Bay. Is it far?"

Marianne's head tilts to the side as a wistful expression takes her over. "Not crazy far. You'd love Apple Blossom Bay. It's this cute little coastal town. Plenty of fishing, great seafood restaurants. Lots of little shops." She smiles. "I love that Logan and his dad do stuff like that. So cute. They deserve a getaway. Plus, the body wasn't found in Sweetwater Falls. The Hamshire police are dealing with that headache."

The Bravery Bakery's kitchen smells like a sugary haven, complete with a giant mixing bowl filled with fudge frosting. Everything in my business comes together to gift me the sweetness I have been searching for my whole life.

To be discussing Jeremy Johnson in this perfect place is less than ideal.

I shut the refrigerator door with a sigh. "Yes, but my job as your best friend is to make sure nothing gives you a headache. I want this murder solved so Jeremy gets out of here and never comes back." I slap my hands together. "Okay, so let's figure this out, starting at the beginning. Jeremy is a giant child who uses another human as his alarm clock. That's our starting point."

Marianne squints one eye at me. "I appreciate the support, but I hardly think you're being objective, here. Isn't that one of the ingredients that makes a good detective?"

I throw my head back, ramping up the theatrics. "Sure,

but I think I should make it crystal clear that he is horrible. Then we can proceed."

Marianne moves her arm out to the side like a floor model. "Your valid opinion has been noted." She snaps the lid back on the bin of sugar.

That's right, instead of a plastic container that could fit in a cupboard, I have a bin the size of a trash can filled with sugar. It's one of the perks of working in my very own commercial kitchen.

The Bravery Bakery was making cupcakes and cake pops out of my Aunt Winifred's kitchen for months, but soon enough, we outgrew the space. My little miracle space is located in the back of Sweetwater Fountains, which used to be a burger joint before the dining area was converted to a storefront that sells handmade fountains and funky jewelry. Jeanette, the owner, had no use for the kitchen, so she leased it to me, alleviating her rent payments and giving me the space to let my confections grow into a business with some serious teeth to it.

I have only been operating out of the new location for a week, so everything still feels like a dream.

The gigantic sugar bin is just one of the many reasons why I smile every day when I come into the kitchen to work at my dream job.

Marianne collects the spatulas and sets them in the sink. "And that's not the beginning, anyway. The start of it could have been when Jeremy was arguing with his manager," she points out.

"Ray," I remind us both. We stuck around only for a few minutes when the police got there. It was just enough time to garner key details of the case.

Marianne nods. "Right. Ray Montagne. Jeremy said there was a contract dispute, but he had that look about him, so you never know." She waves her hand across her face.

"What look?"

Marianne turns her head away from me. "The sort of look that says Jeremy is skirting over something he'd rather not admit to."

I groan as I pick up the mixing bowl and dump it in the sink. "Ugh. This guy. I can't stand him."

Marianne holds up a finger to still my complaining. "Objectivity, Charlotte. It's the quickest way to the truth."

"Oh, fine. But I made it half a minute without mentioning that Jeremy is scum. I think that should count for something."

Marianne grants me a miniature applause for my paltry effort. "Well done. Ray and Jeremy argued, bad enough that others must have heard them, because he was afraid people might assume he killed Ray."

I nod as I start shoving things in the commercial dishwasher, which is my new favorite toy. "Which is why Jeremy didn't just report the crime. He felt the need to drive the dead body across state lines to find Logan."

"Who is still unreachable."

After the dishwasher starts up, I grab a broom and start

sweeping. Now that I have a kitchen all my own, I will not dare let it fall to disrepair. This place is spotless after every day of baking. I have a love for this kitchen, so I take good care of it. I am so grateful that this oasis of sugar and butter exists just for me.

I make sure to sweep out the corners of the kitchen, where sprinkles tend to accumulate. "What do you think Jeremy and Ray were arguing about?"

Marianne puts the carton of eggs in the refrigerator. "And who was the last person to see Ray alive? I have so many questions."

"Who would Ray be fighting with so vehemently that they killed him, and over what?"

"And why move the body? Why bring the body here? Why didn't Jeremy just call the local police?"

I marvel at the polished silver floor. Some might call it plain old gray concrete, but I am certain it is a distinguished silver. "And what was on the piece of paper in Ray's mouth?"

"What piece of paper?" Marianne asks, turning to me when she emerges from the refrigerator.

"Did I not mention?" I explain to her that there was something in between Ray's teeth that looked like it might be a piece of paper. "Whatever is on that paper I'll bet is our next clue."

Marianne's mouth pulls to the side. "How do we get our hands on it? The Hamshire police aren't exactly loose with their evidence handling. I have no right to that information, but that doesn't make me want it less." Then Marianne shakes her head. "No. No, I don't want to know anything about it. Jeremy isn't mine to protect. He is not my fiancé. He's not my boyfriend. He's not my friend. He's not my anything. He got himself into this mess; he can get himself out."

I believe Marianne when she claims she wants nothing to do with this tease of a puzzle. But I also know that every time she thinks of Jeremy, she is reminded of the implosive end to their relationship.

If I want to get Jeremy out of this town so Marianne doesn't have to see him ever again, then I need to know what is written on that piece of paper that was shoved inside of Ray Montagne's mouth.

I might not have access to the information, but I know someone who does.

3

JEREMY'S GIRLFRIEND

*L*ife in Sweetwater Falls has many perks. The slow speed limit means no one is in a hurry to get anywhere. The town is surrounded by nature, so there are plenty of out of towners to keep the small businesses afloat, even in the wintertime. The fact that I work in the back of Sweetwater Fountains means that whenever I get overwhelmed, I can step inside Jeanette's storefront and get myself a healthy dose of serenity.

There are fountains everywhere in the store. From ones taller than me to the smaller tabletop Zen fountains, the entire place is cloaked in calm.

I take a deep breath from my spot at the back exit behind the checkout desk, dragging the sage scent into my lungs. The trickling water of the numerous fountains instills a tranquility I cannot manufacture on my own.

"Have a peaceful day," Jeanette says to her customers as the couple exits the store. She tucks a lock of her waist-length red hair behind her ear as she smiles at me. "I hope your business is going as good as mine today. That is the fourth deluxe fountain I've sold this morning."

"Wow! That's awesome."

I fiddle with the bracelet she gave me last month. It is supposed to infuse me with serenity, but I am listless today, anxious to solve the murder of Ray Montagne, so we can get Jeremy Johnson out of Sweetwater Falls.

I glance around Jeanette's storefront. "Anything I can help with out here?"

Even though I rent the kitchen and don't technically work for Jeanette, I like to make myself useful when my baking is done, and I have a day with nothing on the docket.

Plus, I need a double dose of peace, which I can usually find in Sweetwater Fountains.

"You don't have to do anything but take a break." Jeanette motions to my expression. "You look like you've got something on your mind. Want to talk about it?"

I straighten the bracelets on the rack near the checkout and then set to organizing the chakra stones according to colors of the rainbow. It doesn't suit me to do nothing when I could be helpful. "Marianne didn't want to come out last night. It's fine. I mean, obviously. It's just odd to spend two whole days without her. I asked her if she wanted me to stop by the library today to help shelve books, but she said no. Said she'd be bad company."

Jeanette nods sagely. "That's understandable. What with Jeremy being back in town, I'm sure Marianne is a mix of emotions."

I chew on my lower lip. "I hate that she's in pain and I can't do a thing to stop it. I want Jeremy out of Sweetwater Falls as soon as possible. Can you believe he rented a room at The Snuggle Inn? I have half a mind to ask Fisher to put a laxative in Jeremy's morning coffee."

Though I know this is a bad idea, my mouth pulls to the side as I contemplate calling the head chef at The Snuggle Inn (who just so happens to be like a brother to me after all we've been through) and tell him to do exactly that with Jeremy's coffee.

Jeanette snorts at the suggestion. "I'm sure Fisher could be convinced to make Jeremy's life miserable. There's not a soul in Sweetwater Falls who didn't feel for Marianne. Falling in love with your high school sweetheart who just so happens to have a wandering eye isn't something I would wish on a girl as kind as Marianne." Jeanette taps her temple as a wicked idea occurs to her. "If Jeremy comes in here, I'll try to find a stone that creates chaos to sell to him."

I giggle at Jeanette's vindictive behavior that mirrors my own. "Now you're thinking."

Jeanette pulls her waist-length red hair back as she jots

something down in her ledger. She is wearing a long, moss-colored billowing skirt that makes everything she does look like a fairy-themed work of art.

I decide to make myself useful and grab the duster from behind the desk. I tend to the taller fountains that are harder for her to reach.

When the chime over the door rings, I smile at the new customer while Jeanette frowns at her ledger. "All I know is that no one is happy to see Jeremy in town. Once you cross someone like Marianne, you are not an official citizen of Sweetwater Falls. If tar and feathering was a thing, it would have been a serious consideration."

I vaguely recognize the woman shuffling into the shop as the waitress who took my job when I left my position at Bill's Diner. "Rebecca?" I greet her, trying to recall her name.

"Becca," she corrects me, not unkindly. "Good to see you, Charlotte. I didn't realize you were working at Sweetwater Fountains. I thought you were baking or something like that."

I finish dusting the tall fountain and make my way over to her. "I rent the kitchen in the back of this building. I had some free time, so I came out here to bother Jeanette, talking her ear off while she works." I grin at Becca. "How is Bill's Diner treating you? Is my former boss his usual bucket of sunshine?"

It's a clear joke. Bill rarely reserves a smile for anybody.

Becca motions around the shop. "I came in here for some stress relief, actually. The diner is fine. Bill is grumpy, but I'm learning that isn't anything all that unusual."

Becca graduated from high school last spring. It seems her chipper cheerleader demeanor has not been dimmed by my former boss' sour attitude, which is saying something.

"That's Bill for you. Any reason he's being a downer, or just the usual?"

Becca twirls a lock of her shoulder-length light brown hair around her finger. "He's mad that the diner basically cleared out this morning when Jeremy Johnson came in." She angles her gaze toward Jeanette to include her in the conversation. "I take it you two are sick of having him in town, too?"

Jeanette nods. "Charlotte's plan is to slip him a laxative."

I snort at Jeanette. "Hey, my plan is more sophisticated than just that. I want to solve the murder that brought him here in the first place, which will get him out of town that much faster."

Becca migrates to a fountain that is two feet tall. It is made of concrete bricks and has water flowing over the side and funneling through holes that have been drilled through the center. The well is a light green color, and almost seems to glow with tranquility.

Becca runs her finger through one of the streams of water. "I'm all for that. Bill is frustrating when he's annoyed. Bangs pots and pans in the kitchen. Barks at us to look busy when there's like, one customer in the dining room." She slaps her hands together, spritzing a droplet of water onto her cheek. "So, whodunnit? I'm guessing it was the butler in the library with the candlestick."

I chuckle at her joke. "If only all of this could be as simple as a board game. We don't have much to go on— only a fight with his manager not long before Ray Montagne was found dead in his own car, which isn't all that compelling of evidence. But it spooked Jeremy enough to make him drive across state lines with a dead body in the car, so I'm guessing there's more to the story than the headlines."

Becca's eyebrows raise as she takes out her phone. "Um, yeah. There's a lot more than that. You do know who Jeremy Johnson's girlfriend is, right?"

The way she says his whole name tells me she is more familiar with his stage presence than his time in Sweet-water Falls.

That makes sense, since Becca was still in high school when that whole mess between Marianne and Jeremy blew up.

My nose scrunches. "No. Who is his girlfriend?" I let out a grunt of frustration. "Ugh. I don't want to know, but I do. I don't want any more details of him swimming around in my brain, but if I want him out of here, I need all the facts, so I can figure out who killed Ray. That's the only way to get Jeremy out of Sweetwater Falls."

Becca gives me a wry smile at my logic that is valid both ways. "Jeremy Johnson is dating Melanie Montagne." She gives me a knowing look.

Jeannette frowns. "Is that supposed to mean something to me? I'm so out of touch with pop culture. I don't follow Jeremy's career."

The last name dings in my head. "Melanie Montagne? As in Ray Montagne? The man who was murdered is related to Jeremy's girlfriend?"

Becca chuckles at my astonishment. "You really don't know much about his music, do you. How do you think he made it on a big tour from a small town so quickly? He's hasn't been gone from Sweetwater Falls all that many years. Big successes don't happen overnight." Her eyebrows bounce with innuendo. "Unless, of course, you're dating a woman whose father is a big-time manager for many successful musicians."

My mouth falls open in time with Jeannette setting down her pencil, guffawing in astonishment. "Jeremy is dating the dead man's daughter?"

I piggyback on the tail of her line of thought. "Jeremy had a public argument with his girlfriend's father, and the next time Ray Montagne was seen or heard from was after he died?"

Becca leans on the table beside the fountain she keeps eyeing. "Adds a little more color to the picture, doesn't it? If you want to know more about the kind of person Jeremy Johnson is behind closed doors, I would start by figuring out how to have a conversation with Melanie Montagne. She might know things that her father can no longer tell us." Then she motions to the concrete block fountain. "I think I want to take this one home. Might help me calm down after dealing with Bill's attitude."

Jeannette snaps back to life. "Absolutely. Let me package that up for you. Might you be interested in a bracelet to match the green of the fountain? This jade stone represents wisdom gathered in tranquility. It also brings wealth, which might help, since it sounds like the tips weren't exactly flowing this morning."

I love that Jeanette knows what each gemstone means. I don't have the type of mind that can hold onto details that specific.

Becca nods. "Sure. I could use something cute to distract me from the zero tips that came in while Jeremy Johnson was there. Can you believe he actually expected Bill would comp his meal?" She rolls her eyes. "Thinks that being a celebrity means he doesn't have to pay for food or tip his waitress. He tried to tip me by giving me his autograph." She harrumphs. "I mean, give me a break."

Ugh, this guy. There is not a thing I like about him.

I set about helping Jeanette package up the fountain, since it is a heavy little thing. Becca and Jeanette make idle chatter about the Knit Your Heart Out fair that's coming up, but I cannot engage while my mind is stuck on Jeremy and his girlfriend's dead father.

What was he arguing about? Was it career-related, or did Ray not like that Jeremy was dating his daughter?

I don't know how to go about getting in touch with Melanie Montagne, but I know that would be a good place to start if I am going to solve this thing, so Jeremy can leave Sweetwater Falls once and for all.

4

FLOUR, FROSTING AND FIANCÉ

*M*y baking days are filled with sugar and flour, which find their way onto every surface. The kitchen is cold when I arrive, but after an hour of the ovens cranking out the heat, I am sweating while I work. My cardigan that I wore to work has been discarded in favor of the pale pink t-shirt I had on underneath.

I love the smell of butter, which seems to make everything better. When butter is mixed in with boatloads of sugar? There is nothing better, and certainly nothing that can keep my mood down today.

I haven't invented a flavor of the month yet, but I know that will come when it comes. Last month I had a Christmas cupcake. Peppermint and hot cocoa flavors are a no-brainer for December.

I don't know if it's because January is a little blah with

all the cold and colorless landscape, or if the murder of Ray Montagne is the thing that's getting in the way of my creativity. Perhaps my lack of inspiration is because I haven't been out with Marianne in several days.

My mouth pulls to the side as I tug out a tray of vanilla latte cupcakes from the oven and place them on the stainless-steel countertops. I thought I would get tired of the shine of the silver counters, but each time I polish them at the end of a shift, I love them that much more.

Vanilla latte with a butterscotch buttercream frosting, a vanilla bean cake with a vanilla bean cardamom glaze that's topped with Italian meringue, and a decadent double fudge cupcake make up my normal menu of cupcakes that people can order from my website. The fourth flavor is the flavor of the month, which is...

I'm still not sure.

When the backdoor opens, I expect Marianne to come strolling in. She is a fantastic best friend because she usually helps with the baking whenever she stops by.

But when the most handsome man in the world walks in, clad in his police uniform (as if the angular jaw, the sandy blond hair, and the dimpled chin weren't enough), I startle so badly that I drop the second tray of cupcakes on the floor after they've come out of the oven. The edge of the pan sizzles on my skin, causing me to yelp in pain before I can greet my boyfriend.

Logan grimaces and rushes to my side. "Oh, I saw that.

I should have knocked. I'm sorry, Miss Charlotte. Let's get this under some cold water."

Logan's touch is gentle as he leads me to the large sink and turns on the water, holding my hand under the chilly spray.

"I thought you were coming back later tonight!" I stare up at him, breathless under the weight of his striking features paired with his unpretentious demeanor.

Logan smirks at me, then refocuses on the red of my hand. "That was the plan, but apparently the Hamshire police want my input, since Jeremy will only talk to me."

My elation at seeing Logan crashes under the weight of the mention of Marianne's ex-fiancé. "Ugh. Jeremy is the worst."

Logan chuckles, turning my hand sideways to let the water hit it from a different angle. "That certainly seems to be a popular opinion. How is Marianne holding up?"

"She's not. She's hiding. I haven't seen her in days. She goes to the library and home, and nowhere else. Carlos texted me this morning to ask if I thought he should go over anyway, even though she's told us she wants some time to herself."

Logan presses his lips together while he takes in the news. "What a mess. All of it. Not just Marianne not wanting to go out, but the case itself. Total mess." He jerks his chin over his shoulder. "Not unlike that pile of cupcakes on the floor. Sorry about that."

I shake my head. "It's my fault. You know how I get

around you." I think back to the weeks of clumsy moments I endured when Logan was still new to me. His good looks often stunned me, turning me into a stammering klutz.

Even though we have been dating for a few months now, it seems he still has the ability to startle me into pure inelegance.

Logan keeps one hand on my wrist under the water and curls his other arm around my waist, holding me to him in a way I have been missing. "It's been too long. No offense to my dad, but two sweaty guys smelling like fish and sleeping on cots in the freezing weather doesn't hold a candle to this."

I lean up on my toes and kiss his lips, reminding myself that Logan is not out of my league if I am in his arms. "Thank you for not smelling like fish."

"Took me three showers, but I managed to scrub myself clean."

"I take it you caught a lot of fish?"

Logan smiles at me, looking quite pleased with himself. "I don't like to brag. I'll say I did okay. Apple Blossom Bay is peaceful enough for the fish not to be spooked by out-of-towners."

I bump my hip to his. "You caught a lot, didn't you."

He casts me an impish grin. "I was thinking of frying up a fish tonight for you and Winifred. Do you think if I invited Marianne over for that, it might smoke her out of her funk?"

I nod. "That's a great idea. You're really going to cook for us? I think that's a first. Can't wait."

Logan blows out air through pursed lips with a wary expression, as if bolstering himself for the task. "I'm going to try. That's what the Live Forever Club is all about, right? Taking risks. Karen talked me through a recipe. I had her write it down. Then I made sure she would be available tonight for me to call her to talk me through it over the phone in real time." He gives himself a firm nod. "I can do this. You're going to be so impressed."

I chuckle that he assumes I am never not impressed by him. "I'm already over the moon."

He inhales deeply, just as enraptured by the sugary scent of the kitchen as I am. "I love that frosting you make. You know, the caramel one. So good. I'm glad I got back in time to help with a batch." He motions to the mixer in the corner.

I snicker at his cuteness as I turn off the water and dry my hand off on the nearest towel. "It's not caramel frosting. That's butterscotch buttercream."

Logan shrugs. "It's all the same to me. Caramel, butterscotch. Whatever you call it, I love it."

Now I am invested in this conversation and need to educate this beautiful man. "Butterscotch and caramel are entirely different. Caramel is made with granulated sugar, while butterscotch is made of brown sugar. The taste is night and day."

Logan studies me warily. "Now I'm really nervous to

cook for you tonight. I don't know anything about the spices Karen told me to use."

I chuckle at his conundrum. "I'll make a caramel sauce, so you can taste the difference between that and the butterscotch buttercream. If the fish doesn't smoke Marianne out, then maybe the caramel sauce will."

Logan shrugs. "It's worth a shot." He leans his butt against the counter, crossing his arms over his chest. "Put me to work, Miss Charlotte. I have half an hour before I have to go over to the precinct in Hamshire to deal with Jeremy's mess."

I point to the second mixer. "Do you remember how to make the Italian meringue?"

Logan scoffs. "Are you kidding me? They don't call me the Frosting King for nothing."

I snort at his joke. "You're the only one who calls you that."

"It'll catch on. Just you wait." He gets out the carton of eggs.

Logan may not be the most experienced cook, but he has made the frosting for my cupcakes so many times that I'm sure he could throw together a batch in his sleep.

We work well together, which is no small feat. I need things done a certain way, or the frosting won't come together properly.

"How are things at work?" I ask him, trying not to be obvious in my prying.

"Well, I'm back half a day early, so not great. Carlos

filled me in on the details the report left out. Quite the way to meet Jeremy for the first time. I mean, Marianne obviously traded up when she started dating Carlos. Still, first love and all that. It can't be easy for her to see him."

I know Logan is dancing around the details of the case because I'm not supposed to know things like that, being that I'm a civilian. It is no surprise to me that he skipped to the relational side of things.

My mouth pulls to the side as I set about making another batch of cupcakes to replace the ones I dropped. "I hope Marianne comes over tonight. Getting her out of the house is a good idea."

"I'm making a triple batch of frosting, so you have extra," Logan informs me.

I busy myself picking up the ruined cupcakes off the floor and throwing them in the trash. "Why will Jeremy only talk to you? Are the two of you friends still?"

Logan shrugs. "I guess. I mean, I haven't spoken to him in like, a year. And even then, it wasn't about anything other than his career. But that's always been how Jeremy operates. He's got a big plan and we get to hear about it." He waves his hand in the air to clear it of his obvious unhappiness. "I'm being grumpy. I didn't mean it like that. It's always been a one-sided friendship, but that has more to do with me than him, probably."

"How so?"

Logan shrugs as if he has no idea how to answer my question, but upon further thought, he offers a conjecture that I can tell isn't too off the mark. He stares at the whisk while it whirls in the bowl. "You teach people how to treat you. That's the theory, right? I must've put something out there that told Jeremy our friendship could be all about him. Maybe that's why I wasn't so sad when he moved out of Sweetwater Falls."

I measure the flour while I talk. "You generally have good instincts. If you didn't want to share your life with him, I'm sure you had your reasons."

Logan keeps his eyes on the mixer. "I don't trust him. Never did. He's got this slippery way to him that makes you forget you don't totally agree with what he's doing or what he's saying, but he's joking and smiling, so you think it's just you being a jerk to a nice guy."

I get out the baking soda and salt, measuring out the dry ingredients while I mull over Logan's assessment. "I understand that wariness. Sounds like your gut was spot on, given that he cheated on Marianne."

Logan's upper lip curls. "Before you came along, I mostly stayed out of that drama. But now that I'm dating her best friend, it all hits me closer to the vest. I don't know why Jeremy thinks I am the person he should open up to."

"He still will only talk to you?"

Logan nods as he adds the vanilla extract. "Which makes me think that whatever he's done, it's a whole lot worse than what we're seeing. There aren't that many suspects, I guess, from what the Hamshire police are telling me. Jeremy is the prime person of interest.

Everyone else was in their own trailer around the time of death, surrounded by witnesses who can corroborate their story. It's not looking good."

"Unless Jeremy is the killer, in which case, good job evidence, pointing to the obvious bad guy."

Logan tilts his head to the side, scolding me with a look. "It's hardly enough evidence to convict, and there are plenty of holes in it all. On the one hand, Jeremy reported the body. Guilty people generally don't do that."

"Sure, he reported the body after moving it across state lines."

Logan nods to my fair point. "On the other hand, why doesn't Jeremy have an alibi?"

I sift the powdery ingredients together. "You could always ask his girlfriend."

Logan pauses and turns to me, flicking off the switch on the mixer to give me his undivided attention. "Jeremy has a girlfriend? He might have called her when he discovered the body. She'd be a good person to talk to."

My mouth pulls to the side. "Apparently, Melanie Montagne is Jeremy's girlfriend. Ray's daughter. I would guess if he didn't call Melanie first thing when he found her father dead, he would be a pretty terrible boyfriend."

Logan's mouth falls open. "That wasn't in the report that was sent to me—the fact that Jeremy is dating the victim's daughter. Are you sure?"

"No, but I think it's true. I have no reason to doubt the person who told me. You might want to talk to your buddy

Jeremy and see if you can track down Melanie. I'm sure she's already been notified of her father's death. But it would be interesting to find out if Jeremy contacted her when he found her father's body. And if he didn't, why not?"

Logan stares ahead of him, not focusing his vision while he thinks. "If he called her, she should have phoned the murder into the police. And if Jeremy didn't tell her, that's a complication I can't imagine would be worth the risk. Caring about the image of your own culpability over your girlfriend knowing that her father is dead? That's low." He sighs, pinching the bridge of his nose. "Then again, maybe that's just Jeremy. He does what he wants and expects the rest of the world to just get it."

"He sounds dreamy," I lie, miming barfing on the countertop.

Logan and I bake together for the next twenty minutes until he has to leave. All the while I worry there is far more to this case than Jeremy will ever admit to anyone.

5

VANILLA EXTRACT, PUDDING CUP AND SUGARBEAN

*W*hen I run out of pure vanilla extract, I decide it's time for a trip to the Colonel's General Store. I don't have it in me to make a subpar caramel sauce. If Logan doesn't know the difference between butterscotch and caramel, tonight is the night he gets a proper education on the important things.

I love the giant log cabin look to the Colonel's General Store. It makes me feel like I am walking into a maple syrup advertisement. I am also partial to how meticulously organized this place always is. Everything is stocked in perfect lines. Nothing is dusty or out of date, even though the place has a rustic feel to it.

Aside from pure vanilla extract, I need corn syrup, which shouldn't be too obscure an ingredient to find. But when it's not in the baking aisle, I know I need to scour the shelves because oftentimes items are stocked in odd locations around the store.

I move to the next aisle, going slow so as not to miss anything. The store isn't all that populated midday, but it's not a ghost town, either. I nod to a person whom I know I've seen at the town festivals, but I can't remember their name at the moment.

One day, I will know by name every single person in Sweetwater Falls. Until then, I am known as "Charlotte McKay, the new girl. Winifred's niece."

It's not a bad label, come to think of it.

It's when I meander into the next aisle that my footsteps freeze.

There he is: Jeremy Johnson—scumbag and cheater.

The urge to pick up the nearest can of peas and whip it at his head is strong, but I resist when I hear him talking into his phone. "No, puddin' cup. They shouldn't be calling you. I kept your name out of everything." He pauses, his back to me.

I turn and pick up a can of soup, my gaze fixing on the label so I can stick nearby for this conversation without being too much on his radar.

Jeremy clears his throat into his phone. "It's hard without an alibi. But I know that if I told the police I was with you, it would open up a whole other can of worms. No, no. We said we would keep things quiet, so I didn't give them your name." He sighs like a child being told he can't have dessert. "Come on, Julia. You know it's not like that.

And it's not like I can break up with Melanie now. Her dad just died."

Ice freezes in my veins. Jeremy is sweettalking some "puddin' cup" named Julia when his girlfriend's name is Melanie?

Jeremy just confessed that he was with Julia at the time of Ray's death, which sounds like it would be a solid alibi for him. But he won't tell the police that, because it would out him as being a giant cheater, being with Julia instead of Melanie.

The nerve of this guy. No, he can't have the police knowing that he still is and always will be a cheating, lying dog.

I slam the can back on the shelf and pick up another, glowering at the thing. I will myself not to chuck it at Jeremy, though my hand is itching to do so.

Jeremy ends the call and then makes another. "Hi, sugarbean."

My mouth falls open at the nickname he reserved for Marianne.

Why is Jeremy calling Marianne? How often does he call her? Have they been talking on the phone regularly?

What is she doing, talking to him? Marianne is happy with Carlos. Jeremy smashed her heart. How could she do this to Carlos? How could she do this to herself?

I am dumbstruck and so lost in my thoughts that I don't hear any of the rest of their conversation.

In fact, when Jeremy ends his call and strolls past me, I

miss the opportunity to trip him. I forget my mission for being at the Colonel's General Store completely and freeze in the middle of the aisle.

I can only hope that my best friend doesn't shoot herself in the foot by going after the man who broke her heart.

6

CARAMEL AND CARLOS

*D*inner shouldn't be a tense affair, but I can't make my smile natural. The cupcakes turned out exceptionally well because I do my best baking when I am stressed.

When Marianne comes through the front door, my natural inclination should be to wrap my arms around my best friend. I haven't seen her in four days, which is a world record for us. But I know I'm smiling weird when I greet her.

"It's good to see you."

My Great Aunt Winifred is ninety years old, but she is more spritely and graceful than I am in this moment. She kisses Marianne's cheek, her eyes crinkling with a welcoming smile. "Come on in, dear. Let me take your coat. You'll catch your death out there if the weather keeps throwing a snow fit." She shivers even as she shuts the door behind Marianne. "How are you, honey?"

Marianne casts us both a wan smile. "I've been better. Thanks for inviting me over. I needed my space, but tonight I really just wanted to get out of my own head."

"Makes sense," I offer, though I should be talking her head off.

I don't understand why she would get back with Jeremy, but I do know that when I am turned around, I would want to be accepted and love, even when I make foolish choices.

I lace my fingers through hers as we walk into the cheery, yellow kitchen.

Marianne turns her head this way and that, taking in the set table without any food in sight. "I thought Logan was frying up the fish that he caught."

"He is," I assure her. "He just called to say he's running late. He's on his way. In the meantime, we get to catch up."

Aunt Winnie moves to the pink carryout box that bears my business' logo. "If either of you are opposed to having dessert before dinner, I don't want to hear it. Life is for the living, and cupcakes are for the eating."

Marianne toasts Winifred with an imaginary glass. "Hear, hear."

Marianne looks like she hasn't slept well. Her hair is not brushed, and she doesn't have the usual pixie pep in her step.

I lead her to the dining table in the kitchen where we sit while Winifred pops open the top of the box.

I love the sound of her gasp as it fills the kitchen. "Oh, Charlotte! What did you do?"

I give my great aunt half a smile. "Logan doesn't know the difference between butterscotch and caramel, so I thought I would educate him. Can't have him not understanding the finer things in life."

Winifred sits with us at the table after turning on the stove to heat the kettle. "I'll need some tea with this. Oh, I can already tell I'm going to love it. Talk me through the flavors."

I peel off the wrapper of the nearest one and set it on the table in front of me. Though I made them today, I haven't tried a bite yet. "It's an applesauce cinnamon cupcake. The peanut butter buttercream has a kick of cloves to cut the sweetness. Then I crushed pretzels and made caramel corn for the topping."

Aunt Winifred inhales the intoxicating salty-sweet scent. "I love my life. I can't imagine it gets better than this. Please never stop letting me be your taste tester."

I chuckle at her girlish glee. "Deal."

I love watching people take their first bite of my cupcakes. The "mm" noise followed by the inhale and then the exhale is just about my favorite sound in the world. To know that I did that—I brought joy to the people I love—is no small honor.

Aunt Winnie and Marianne don't disappoint.

Marianne's eyes roll back. So distracted by the flavors is she that she doesn't seem to care that she has pretzels crumbs peppering her lips. "Charlotte, this is the only thing worth coming out of the house for. If I tell you I'm depressed, will you make a dozen of these for me?"

I reach across the table to place my hand atop hers. "Talk to me. I will happily ply you with a million cupcakes if it helps you open up."

Aunt Winnie pats the top of my hand, which rests atop Marianne's. "We're listening, Marianne. We've got the perfect cupcakes, tea brewing and four ears aimed your way."

Marianne sets her cupcake down, but not before plucking off a piece of caramel corn from the top and munching on it. "Mm. Even your caramel corn is better than any I've ever had. Can you teach me how to make that? I could eat a bucket of the stuff."

I nod, inching my chair closer. "Anything you need."

Marianne stares at the cupcake in lieu of meeting our careful stares. "It's weird having Jeremy back in town. I don't want him here. But that's selfish. I mean, it's not like I own this town."

Aunt Winnie squeezes Marianne's wrist. "You want him gone?"

Marianne nods. "I hate what this is doing to me. Just knowing he's in the city makes me all mousy and quiet. I like that I laugh out loud now. I love that I'm Marianne the Wild. I've changed so much since I was engaged to him. Yet he's in town for not even a whole week, and I've clammed up, completely forgetting who I am."

Aunt Winnie thumps her fist on atop the table. "So, it's decided. Anyone who takes away your wildness has to go."

Marianne chuckles at Winifred's matter-of-fact ruling. "It's not that Jeremy has done anything this week to take away my wildness. I mean, I've been hiding out for the most part. He's done nothing wrong."

"Other than possibly murder his manager," I mumble.

Marianne lowers her chin. "I hate that he has this hold over me. All it takes is a mention of him and I'm all turned around. I don't want to talk to Carlos, because I'm embarrassed that Jeremy has any sort of effect on me at all. I don't know how to talk to Carlos about it, so I've been shutting him out. Avoiding his phone calls."

Aunt Winnie casts me a "yikes. This is worse than I thought," sort of look before she addresses Marianne. "I'm not sure that's your best move. Is Carlos devoid of ex-girlfriends? I'm sure he would feel strange if one showed back up in his hometown with some sort of scandal chasing him around."

Marianne nods noncommittally. "I guess. I want this to be over. I want Jeremy to go back to his fancy country music star life with his big city-bred girlfriend, so I never have to think about him again." She runs her palm over her face. "Of course, I still will think about him. Just the mention of him makes me feel small and inept. Like I'm some small-town joke."

My nostrils flare as I try to keep my raging temper under control. "You are not small or inept. Are you kidding me? You're the head librarian! You run that place. And you're not a joke. Do you know how hard it's been to spend these few days without you? It's been awful! You are none of those things, Marianne. Jeremy is awful. Wonderful people make no sense to the terrible ones who don't know the treasure they have."

Aunt Winifred smiles at the two of us. "I'm inclined to agree, though I might be biased. You take as long as you need to feel down. Before you know it, Jeremy will be gone. Best not ignore Carlos while you're fishing for meaning in all of this. Carlos is a good one. Might not want to make the good one suffer because of the bad one."

I take in Aunt Winnie's advice for Marianne, mulling over her wisdom. I truly hope that Marianne learns she can trust Carlos with the icky parts of her past. If not, I fear that Jeremy will be the only man on her mind, and he certainly does not deserve a pedestal like that.

"A double date," I insist, doing all I can to push her away from flirty phone calls with Jeremy, wherein he calls her "sugarbean". I want to remind Marianne of the quality man she has who would never leave her high and dry. "Logan's back in town now. Let's go out, the four of us. It's been a hot minute since Logan and I have ruined a movie with serious talk."

Marianne casts me a wan smile. "That sounds nice. I

don't care what movie we see, unless it has cheating in it. I don't think I can stomach that at the moment."

I bite my tongue to keep from asking her if she feels guilty about the phone calls with her ex-fiancé, and how she would feel if Carlos was sneaking around while she was pining for him and giving him his requested space.

I keep my thoughts to myself, hoping Marianne will come to her senses on her own, before she loses Carlos for good.

7

FOOD POISONING

$\mathcal{N}$either Aunt Winnie nor I are moving with all that much pep in our steps the morning after Logan's fish fry.

I brew Aunt Winnie some tea as the doorbell rings. "Does your stomach feel a little sloshy?" I ask her, moving slowly toward the front door so she doesn't have to get up.

Aunt Winnie nods. "I thought something tasted off in the fish last night, but Logan's so charming that I didn't question it like I should have."

I groan as my hand hits the doorknob. "Food poisoning?"

Aunt Winnie's reply is just as grim. "I'm afraid so."

I open the door to Agnes' chipper morning smile. "Hello, Charlotte, dear. Normally I would let myself in, but I've got my hands full." She displays to me her armloads of yarn spilling out of various bags.

"Oh, let me take that for you. Come on in and get out of the cold." I shiver at the gust of wind that accompanies the white flakes falling from the sky.

It's barely eight o'clock in the morning and nature has already been hard at work, decorating the landscape with sparkling white.

I juggle the bags of yarn as I set them on the floor of the living room next to the mauve couch. "Are you clearing out your crafting room?" I ask her, amazed that one person can own this much yarn. "Or did you buy out a craft store?"

Agnes chortles at me. Her white curls are pinned around her face, giving me a full view of her pink lips that match the tip of her chilled nose. "Oh, no. This isn't even half the stuff. I've got more in my trunk."

"I'll get it. You sit down and warm up. I've got the kettle on. When I get back in, I'll fix you a cup of tea."

Though I have no energy for such things, and my stomach feels like it might empty itself at any moment, I know that I can't in good conscience ask a senior citizen to empty her trunk on a blustery morning like this.

My movements are slow as I toe my boots on and pull my winter coat over my shoulders. No part of me wants to be outside. If I'm being honest, no part of me wants to be out of bed.

I amble to Agnes' trunk, expecting a few extra bags, at most. My mouth falls open when a crate of knitting pattern books is accompanied by no less than a dozen bags of yarn.

Colors of all sorts shout out at me, telling me they are ready to have some fun and be made into something snuggly. I can't imagine how many blankets this collection would make.

It takes me three trips to get everything into the house, including the slow cooker filled with chicken noodle soup that was set on the floor of the front seat. By the time I get my boots off and hang up my coat, I am regretting my choice to get out of bed.

The kettle sings before I can set to organizing Agnes' things, so I slump into the kitchen, set the slow cooker on the counter, and go about fixing a pot of tea. "What brings the Queen of the Yarn to us this morning?"

Agnes bustles about the kitchen until she locates a sleeve of saltine crackers. "Winnie called this morning and told me you two were feeling under the weather, so I came here to help out. I've got a fair amount of soup made, but I didn't have saltines. Munch on these until your stomachs can handle the good stuff." She lifts the lid off the slow cooker and inhales the fragrant broth. "Homemade chicken noodle soup. I always keep a chicken carcass in the freezer in case Winnie, Karen or Marianne comes down with anything. And now you, of course, Charlotte dear."

My appreciation stales on my tongue before regret sweeps over me. "Oh, Marianne! She had the food, too. So did Logan. I should call them."

Agnes nods. "Absolutely. Call Marianne and I'll go pick

her up. Logan, too. They can't be expected to look after themselves if it's food poisoning we're up against."

I groan, wishing I didn't have to call Logan to ask him if he has food poisoning. "Maybe we have the flu?" I suggest. "That's possible."

Aunt Winnie shakes her head. "I think this came from the fish, honey cake. I hate to say it because you know I love Logan, but that fish tasted off to me." She shakes her head. "It's always the cute ones. Good cop, bad chef."

I motion to the pot of soup after I plug in the slow cooker to keep it warm. "You did all this for us this morning? You're here to take care of us?"

Agnes tilts her head at me as if there should be no question to this obvious fact. Compassion shimmers in her green eyes. "Of course. Winnie and Karen are my best friends. You and Marianne are my little sisters. If you're sick, where else would I be?"

Moisture pools in my eyes because I have never known such kindness. I'm sure my mother opened a can of soup when I was a child, but after your adolescence, when you're sick, you figure it out on your own. To be taken care of when you don't have the wherewithal to do more than get out of bed is a gift I do not take for granted.

Agnes takes in my burgeoning emotion and scoops me into her arms, her soft lips pressing to my cheek with a sweet kiss. "There, there, Charlotte the Brave. I'll go out and fetch Marianne and Logan, and we'll set up camp here. I'll call Karen for reinforcements."

Normally the Live Forever Club drives golf carts, but in the winter months, Agnes is the only one with her driver's license still intact, so she is the chauffeur when I am unavailable.

"You don't have to do that. I can go get them." Though, as I say this, I'm not sure I should be that far away from a toilet.

Agnes waves away my offer. "It's done. Call Logan and see how bad off he is. I'll check in with Marianne."

I nod and grab up my phone, plopping down in the chair at the kitchen table while I wait for the call to connect.

Logan answers with a groan, which seals it.

Aunt Winnie and I don't have the flu. It's definitely food poisoning.

"How are you feeling, Logan?" I ask him with empathy sweetening my tone.

Logan groans again. "I'm dying. My stomach is trying to leave my body. I'm a sinking ship."

I chuckle at his dramatic phrasing. "Poor thing. Winnie and I aren't feeling too hot, either. Agnes is on her way to pick up Marianne and bring her here. Then she's coming for you."

"Huh? No, don't send Agnes. I don't want anyone to see me like this."

Agnes holds out her hand expectantly after wrapping up her quick call to Marianne. The moment I hand the phone over, her business face kicks into high gear. "I'm coming over in ten minutes, Logan. The four of you have food poisoning, so I'm bringing you all here to look after you."

I can hear his reply. "I don't want Charlotte to see me like this, Agnes. This is why I don't cook! I can't believe I gave everyone food poisoning!"

"Pish posh. No one cares how it happened. We only care that you're okay."

"I have to go into work in ten minutes, Agnes. Thanks for the offer, but I can't take a day off. I just came back from vacation and there's a murder investigation I need to be there for. Jeremy won't talk to anyone but me."

"Does he know you have food poisoning?"

"I called him this morning, letting him know I would be late, so yeah."

Agnes' maternal expression mutates to a glower. "Jeremy Johnson is the most selfish person I have ever met. Making you work when you're sick? I never. Though, I'm not sure what I should expect, given his past behavior. He won't talk to anyone but you, even though you should be in bed?"

"Yeah. It's fine. I did this to myself. And to Winnie, Marianne and Charlotte. I can't believe I gave my girlfriend food poisoning!"

Agnes' tone turns kind once more. "I've got the girls. I'll take good care of them here. Don't you worry about them. Stay hydrated, understood?"

"I can't keep anything down. Not even water," he whines.

My heart goes out to him. I wish I could be there to make it all better.

Though, if I'm wishing for anything, I should probably also wish for Marianne, Aunt Winnie and myself to get better, too.

Agnes talks him through the basics of care when one has food poisoning, and then ends the call, shaking her head at the phone. "If I've never said so, I'll make my feelings clear now: I can't stand Jeremy. He doesn't care about anyone but himself, making Logan go to work in his condition." She stomps to the front door and puts her coat back on. "I'll be back soon, sweethearts. Marianne said she's too sick to get out of bed. I'm going to take Karen to Marianne's, so she can look after our little librarian there. Then I'll be back. Drink that tea and don't do anything strenuous while I'm out."

Once Agnes is gone, Aunt Winnie stirs her tea, blowing on the cup while I lay my forehead on the table to cool it. "I'm not one for letting people walk over the ones I love," she comments, thinking out loud.

"I'm all for running Jeremy out of town. I just need my stomach to settle down before I grab up my pitchfork." My body is tired and worn, so my words go out unchecked. I turn my face, so my cheek is pressed to the table. "Aunt Winnie, I have to tell you something."

My great-aunt stills, locking her eyes onto me. "Why do I get the feeling I should be bracing myself?"

I keep my face pressed to the tabletop. "I overheard Jeremy on his phone yesterday while I was in the Colonel's General Store. He was talking to a woman on the phone who was not his girlfriend. Someone named Julia. He said they couldn't tell Melanie about their secret now, since her father just died, even though it would clear his name in the murder case."

Winnie slams her fist to the table. "Weasel!"

I agree wholeheartedly. "There's more. After he hung up with her, he called someone else. He sounded all cutesy, calling the woman on the phone 'sugarbean'." I pause, swallowing hard, though I can tell Aunt Winnie is already reaching the same conclusion. "'Sugarbean' was his nickname for Marianne."

Aunt Winnie's pallor is already paler than it should be, but she goes positively ashen now. "No. Marianne isn't taking back up with Jeremy again. I don't believe it."

"I don't want to believe it, either, but I know what I heard. That's why last night I floated the idea of going on a double date with Logan and Carlos. I don't want her cheating on Carlos the way Jeremy cheated on her. I can't believe she would do that, but I know what I heard."

Aunt Winnie's mouth firms. "That settles it. I was holding back because I wanted things to play out naturally. I was hoping Jeremy would fade away once this whole mess with the dead body was over. But I think it's time to take matters into our own hands."

I lift my head, my eyes wide. "What do you mean?"

Aunt Winnie picks up her phone and finds Karen's number. "We're going to make Jeremy wish he never came back to Sweetwater Falls. It's time to bring in the professionals."

I have no idea what that could entail, but the stalwart look of vengeance on Aunt Winifred's face is not one I am capable of questioning.

Whatever is about to happen, I am glad I am not on the receiving end of the Live Forever Club's wrath.

8

KNITTING AND PLOTTING

*N*ever let it be said that sweet old ladies are pushovers—especially not the Live Forever Club. Every time Aunt Winnie, Marianne or I get up from our spots on the couch, Agnes is there to sit us back down. Agnes has set up her knitting station in the living room "so she can keep an eye on us."

It's the sweetest kind of hovering I have ever experienced.

Agnes has a pen and paper on the end table by her side while she knits. "I don't think it's enough. Putting sugar in his gas tank? Teenagers do that. Plus, we want him out of town, not stuck in town."

Aunt Winnie's mouth pulls to the side. We are both sweating in between our trips to the bathroom while Agnes whistles away, knitting her heart out.

"I'm not my most devious when I'm sick," Aunt

Winifred admits. "I'll have better ideas for how to run Jeremy out of town when I'm not trying to convince my stomach to calm down."

Agnes hands me two spare knitting needles and nods at me. "Give it a try. I find knitting unwinds my mind. Helps me think. We're going for misery when it comes to Jeremy, not inconvenience."

I hold the two long needles in my fist with a hapless expression crossing my features. "You have to know I don't know how to knit. Like, not even close. I tried a tutorial online a few years ago and ended up throwing a knitting needle across the living room."

Agnes chortles. "You didn't have me back then. And sometimes throwing a knitting needle is exactly what the situation calls for."

She shows me how to hold the two needles, limp wristed but with purpose. Then we go over how to tie a slipknot over and over, undoing it and redoing it until I get it perfect without making it too tight.

Then things really get going. My stomach is a brick of discomfort but learning how to make a row of stitches distracts me just enough from my pain.

Of course, the entire first row, I learn after I complete it, is too tight, so I have to undo the entire thing, then redo it with a looser pull on the yarn.

"This is hopeless," I whine to Agnes. "I'm not going to be an accomplished knitter. At this point, tying my own shoes seems like a chore."

Agnes' smile never falters, nor does her patience wane. She talks me through the stitching in between us throwing out ideas of how to make Jeremy miserable enough to leave Sweetwater Falls. We want him to stay in Hamshire instead through the duration of the investigation. They can question him just as well over there.

The tip of my tongue pokes between my lips. "We could always tell him he's won a trip to Sally's Beauty Barn and slip Sally a little something extra to shave his head," I suggest, picturing the arrogance of his blond coif.

Winifred chuckles. "I like that. Sally can be persuaded. Her ex-husband cheated on her. I'll bet she could go for a little revenge by proxy."

I guffaw, horrified that anyone might cheat on that sweet woman. "I didn't know she was married before, or that her ex-husband was such a dufus."

Agnes coos while she studies her stitches. "Dufus, eh? I think we can work up a stronger word than that. He left Sally for her sister." She shakes her head. "We took her out a few times when it all blew up. Poor thing. So yes, that goes on the list. Sally's in." Agnes jots down a dastardly haircut from Sally on the pad of paper on the end table by her side. "Come to think of it, that might be an untapped asset when it comes to chasing Jeremy out of town. Anyone who values not being cheated on because they've experienced the horror firsthand would be helpful."

Aunt Winnie holds up her finger. "Fisher's girlfriend cheated on him about two years back. Remember her?"

Agnes nods. "Oh, yes. What can Fisher do for us?"

I mull over the plethora of possibilities. "Well, Jeremy is staying at The Snuggle Inn. I suggested laxatives in the coffee but being that I have an intimate relationship with the toilet today, that might be too mean."

Aunt Winifred shakes her head. "No such thing. I think we should have Logan cook for him. Logan put the leftovers from the fish fry in my fridge. I didn't have the stomach to look at the food again, so I haven't thrown it out yet."

I shouldn't laugh. I mean, I am in some serious pain from food poisoning. I shouldn't wish that on Jeremy.

Then again...

I set down my knitting on my lap. "If Jeremy doesn't care that Logan has food poisoning, then perhaps a special delivery of food straight from his old friend would be in order."

Aunt Winnie chuckles darkly. "I love it. And when Marianne is back on her feet, let's make sure to book up her time. I don't want her spending a second with him. Jeremy is a charmer, that's for sure, but he's horrible. He'll seduce her and then throw her out once his name is cleared and he's back on tour with his fancy pants band."

My mouth pulls to the side while I check the looseness of my stitching. "Unless Jeremy is guilty, in which case Marianne is falling for a murderer."

Agnes stops knitting, staring at us as we all take this

problem a bit more seriously. "We won't let that happen," Agnes assures us.

By hook or most definitely by crook, we are determined to keep Marianne away from Jeremy, so she doesn't become the next dead body he comes across.

9

BAD FISH, COFFEE AND CLOTHING

*A*fter two days of nothing but saltines and Agnes' miracle chicken soup, finally Winifred, Marianne and I are back on our feet.

The sound of the mixer soothes me while the scent of sugar fills the kitchen. My stomach is still tender, but my nose is ready for action. The sweetness has depth to it, and the cinnamon cuts the tartness of the apples so the new flavor of the month cupcakes aren't one-dimensional. They have plenty of flavors that unfold as the dessert hits various parts of the person's tongue.

I also love that there is more than one texture, too. There is the crunch of the caramel corn on top, and the soft bite of the cinnamon cupcake. Peanut butter buttercream can be too sweet for my liking, so a dash of cloves really sets this frosting apart.

My kitchen smells like a hug.

I have far more orders for the flavor of the month than anything else on my menu. In fact, the applesauce cupcake with peanut butter buttercream, topped with pretzels and caramel corn comprises two-thirds of the orders placed online.

I don't have the energy to dance around my giant kitchen, but my spirits are light enough to wish my body could attempt something so spirited.

When the backdoor opens, I smile when I see that Logan is finally out of bed and on his feet. There is decidedly less pep in his step, but it's good to see his complexion isn't the sallow green it was when I went to visit him yesterday and drop off more of Agnes' soup.

"You're looking much better," I tell Logan, kissing his cheek.

"I'm halfway to feeling like myself again, which is a far cry better than I was doing yesterday. Remind me never to cook for you again. Nothing but sandwiches and pizzas. Those are the two things I am good at. None of this high-stakes cooking, where if I do something wrong, I give the people I'm trying to impress an unhealthy dose of food poisoning. Definitely not my best foot forward."

"It's water under the bridge. Though, I'm not sure Aunt Winnie will let you cook anything more than canned soup from here on out."

"Fine by me. Karen came over last night and figured out where I went wrong. Still, I don't trust myself. I'll do the catching of the fish, and Karen can do the frying. Other than that, I'm out."

I chuckle at the proverbial tail wagging between his legs. "Poor Logan. And you had to work all week while you were sick? You've suffered enough. Best not beat yourself up about it."

"Well, I was supposed to work today, and I'm actually feeling okay enough to do so, but now Jeremy is sick, so I can at least take a long lunch to come and see you." He slaps his palms together. "So put me to work. I know you're behind, given that my fish put you out of commission for half the week."

I love that he came over to be kind to me. It warms me all the way to my toes that he cares enough about me and my business to come over on his break and help out. I don't know how I got so lucky.

"Jeremy's been anxious to talk to me every time we've met up, but today he's a no-show. It's weird." Logan grabs the mixing bowl and starts making butterscotch buttercream frosting for one of my staple cupcake offerings, since he has deemed himself the Frosting King. He wants no part of the actual baking, but mixing ingredients together is right up his alley.

I keep my eyes from Logan while I measure out the baking soda. "Um, I might know why he didn't show up at the precinct for your meeting."

Logan turns slowly to me. "How would you know that?"

I chew on my lower lip as guilt creeps in and taps me on the shoulder. "I mean, I don't know for sure, but it might have something to do with a delivery from…" I shake my head. "It doesn't matter who it's from. But some of the leftovers from the lovely meal you made us might have found their way over to Jeremy at The Snuggle Inn. You know, since he's been on the road for so long, perhaps he could use a homecooked meal prepared by his old bestie."

Logan closes his eyes and lowers his chin. "Are you kidding me? The generous donor wouldn't happen to be a member of the Live Forever Club, would she?"

I bite down harder on my lower lip and shrug. "I mean, it's possible. I couldn't say for sure."

Logan tsks me. "I can't believe I didn't throw out those leftovers. I packaged them up and left them with Winifred. Now I can add Jeremy to the list of people I've poisoned. Awesome."

I rush to try and smooth things over. "I'm sure he didn't eat the whole meal. He has Fisher cooking for him, so I'll bet he only had a bite or two."

Logan casts me a dubious look. "I sure hate to think of what you deviants are capable of if I ever get on your bad side."

"You'll never have to worry about that, because you wouldn't propose to Marianne and then leave her high and dry while cheating on her." I grumble while I measure out the salt. "And you wouldn't come back into town with a dead body in your backseat, then cheat on your current girlfriend with your former fiancée."

Logan gapes at me. "What? Did I hear that right?"

I nod slowly. "Unfortunately, you did. So, I don't know what your plans are for Friday night, but if we could go on a double date with Marianne and Carlos, that would be good. Anything to get her away from Jeremy."

He glares at the butter as he dumps it into the bowl. "Of course. I can't believe Marianne would fall for Jeremy again. After all he put her through... Man, I didn't see that coming. Yes, let's go out tomorrow night. Doesn't Marianne know he's most likely a murderer?"

I still. "I think we're all hoping he's guilty, but other than his stupidity and penchant for bad choices, we don't have enough proof. You're the one who said as much."

Logan keeps his eyes on the powdered sugar as he measures some out and dumps it in the bowl. "That's because you don't know what was stuffed in Ray's mouth when his body was brought in."

I abandon my ingredients, my attention fully on Logan. "Are you going to keep me in suspense? Tell me what you found. I saw there was a white something in there, maybe a piece of paper, but I didn't fish it out or anything."

Logan keeps his eyes on his work. "Well, the coroner did. Turns out, Ray Montagne had one of his musicians' contracts shoved in his mouth. A final 'screw you', if you will."

I close my eyes. "Dare I ask whose contract it was?"

"One guess."

I fold my arms across my chest. "That feels like proof to me. Can you lock Jeremy up and throw away the key?"

"Not yet. And it's not conclusive evidence. Anyone could have shoved the contract in Ray's mouth. It's a good idea if you want to frame Jeremy."

I spread my arms out. "Who would want to frame Jeremy?"

Logan shoots me a look as if to ask if I'm trying to be funny. "Well, it turns out that list is pretty long. Apparently not everyone on the tour was thrilled to see Jeremy in the number two spot for the shows. He was supposed to be the opener for two bigger bands. But he was put in the middle of the lineup and was given a longer set time. Neither band was happy. The one who had to be the opener was upset because they have a bigger following and draw more ticket sales. The main attraction band was upset because they said it felt like Jeremy shortcut his way to the top. He didn't put in the years of hard work they put in to get where they were."

I lean on the countertop, trying to keep up with a life that is completely out of my depth. "How exactly does one shortcut their way to the top?"

Logan gives me a knowing look. "Might want to ask Melanie Montagne—Ray's daughter and Jeremy's girlfriend. Though, if Jeremy is leading on Marianne, I can't imagine Melanie will be his girlfriend for much longer." He closes his eyes and lets out a grunt of frustration. "Why does Jeremy think I am okay with this? Why would he come back and insist on talking with me, knowing that Marianne and I are friends? Jeremy and I were never particularly close."

I migrate to Logan's side and rest my hand atop his. "Because you are a good person. That's why Jeremy came to you. He knew you would listen to him. Whether or not he tells the truth is an entirely different matter. But it's no secret you're good at your job. And you're a quality person even off the job. Of course Jeremy would seek you out when he's all turned around and needs people to listen to him."

Logan's shoulders sag. "You're good at this—being kind to me. Thank you. I was thinking Jeremy sought me out because he thinks I'm a sucker who will fall for his lies."

Well, that might be part of it.

But I don't say that aloud. Instead, I rub Logan's arm. "What's the next step? I mean, it's a big deal to have Jeremy's contract inside the dead man's mouth."

Logan shrugs. "I'm consulting on this because Jeremy will only speak to me. I don't want to stick my nose where it doesn't belong and make everyone miserable."

My mouth pulls to the side. "I mean, if it was me, I would want to know what's on that contract. Yes, the fact that it was shoved in Ray's mouth is a big thing on its own, but why? Why would it be Jeremy's contract? I would think it would be easier to frame Jeremy with a piece of his clothing or something like that. And if it was Jeremy behind the murder, then there was something on that paper that made him angry enough to shove it down Ray's throat."

Logan meets my gaze. "We need to see what's on that paper."

I nod, crossing my arms over my chest. "And it wouldn't hurt you to question Jeremy about the contract, too. Will he tell you he was happy with his contract? That would be good to know."

Logan leans his hip against mine. "If he wasn't happy with his contract, that's a good way to let Ray know." He kisses my temple, infusing my whole body with a peace that's hard to reach on my own when such topics are bandied about. "Thanks. I think I needed to talk that out. I'll go to The Snuggle Inn first thing tomorrow to ask Jeremy about the contract."

My gaze cuts away from him. "You're going to The Snuggle Inn?"

"It's better than waiting for Jeremy to come to me."

I try to comb the culpability from my features. "You might want to steer clear of any coffee he has sent to his room. Not unless you want to get reacquainted with your old pal, the toilet."

"Miss Charlotte," Logan scolds me.

"And you might want to stay away from him if he's had his clothes cleaned and delivered. I can't tell you how I know this, but there might just so happen to be itching powder sprinkled on his clothing. So, you know, you might want to go with handshakes instead of hugs."

Logan shakes his head at me, tsking my bad behavior. "Well, at least I know not to cross you. I don't know what Jeremy is thinking, messing with Marianne again like that. And I don't know what she's thinking, sneaking around with him when Carlos is a good guy who is absolutely smitten with her."

I can't hazard a guess as to why Marianne would give Jeremy a second look. But it makes sense to me that Jeremy would realize he lost someone truly spectacular, and scramble to get them back.

I can only hope Marianne confronts her conscience before it's too late. I don't want my best friend to end up attached to a man who is destined for jail.

10

JEREMY'S BEVERAGE

*T*he next morning has me hanging out with Fisher in the kitchen of The Snuggle Inn. When he heard I had food poisoning, he sent over a quart of potato soup he swore would soak up anything in my stomach that shouldn't be there.

Fisher is a good friend, so every now and then, I return the favor and pop in on him in the kitchen of the local bed and breakfast to offer him a hand, since I know he often works back there alone.

"What a mess," Fisher complains. "Everyone wants to eat at The Snuggle Inn this week. People from out of town have been making reservations all week long in hopes of catching a glimpse of our local country music star." Fisher rolls his eyes. "No one from Sweetwater Falls is impressed with him, so it's all out of towners in need of some good gawking. I swear, I've never seen so many dishes go cold because they're staring at a grown man in a cowboy hat." He grumbles to himself. "I usually send Lydia a pick-me-up tea and biscuit while she works the front desk, but I haven't even been able to do that."

"That sounds annoying. But how great that you're booked up. That's nice. It's got to be good for business."

"It is, sure, but my paycheck stays the same, so I'm not as thrilled as Lenny, the owner. Instead, I get double the work and not an inch more help to deal with it all."

Fisher's forearms are huge and peppered with black hair to match his curls on top. His hair has been slicked back and tucked into a bandana. His round face has a thin sheen of sweat across it, which tugs at my soft spots.

I motion to the cutting board before me. "Give me more to do. I'm only chopping vegetables."

Which just so happens to be my specialty. When I lived in Chicago before I moved to Sweetwater Falls, I worked at a restaurant doing salad prep, which is essentially chopping vegetables all day long.

"Are you kidding me? That's exactly the help I need. I can handle the other stuff. I'm behind on prep, so you are a godsend." He frowns at me. "And you probably came here to hang out. You're not here to listen to me whine."

I chuckle at him. "You call that whining? Pathetic. Put your heart into it, Fish. Really sell your misery to the cheap seats. I'm starting to think you like being shorthanded."

Fisher throws his head back while he stirs a pot of

soup. "Waaaaaa! I don't like when minor league celebrities come to the Inn! I'm an old man who likes steady work, not a deluge."

"That's more like it. Now I almost believe you're inconvenienced." I scoff at him again. "And forty is hardly old."

Fisher snorts while he stirs. "I'm glad you're here. Having the extra pair of hands aside, it's good to see you out and about. And I can't wait to try the new cupcake you brought me. I love that I get to be your taste-tester."

"Yes, and one of these days you'll have to learn how to give me unbiased feedback." I shoot him a squinty eye.

Fisher grins at me. "What about 'it's perfect, brilliant and will make all other cupcakes cry' is unbiased? I mean, honestly."

One of the servers comes into the kitchen, looking winded. "Jeremy Johnson is in the dining room. Brace yourself for everyone ordering what he wants, which is a bowl of broth and some bread."

I try to keep my smug expression to myself. "Sounds like he's not feeling well. Shame."

Fisher eyes me after the waitress exits. "Uh-huh. Don't think I didn't see Agnes come by with a to-go container full of food for him. I know how you ladies work. He screwed over Marianne, so you've all set out to make his life miserable." He holds up his hand. "And before you ask, yes, I put a laxative in his coffee. I even went so far as to put activated charcoal in his afternoon tea to stain his teeth black. I hope the town enjoys the sight of that."

I put down the knife and offer up a slow clap. "Hail to the chief."

He tips his head to accept the applause. "Break Marianne's heart, you get to walk around with black teeth. I think that should be obvious."

"You are dangerous, Sir."

"I'll take that as a compliment. My aim in life is to one day be able to keep up with the antics of the infamous Live Forever Club. I'll get there—one malfeasance at a time."

I glare at the door as if Jeremy should be able to feel the heat of my stare and whither under the weight of my disapproval. "I wish I could give Jeremy a piece of my mind."

Fisher motions to the door, where the dining area is just on the other side. "Well, he's right out there. It's not like I'm going to stop you. Bonus points if you knock that stupid cowboy hat off his head."

I give Fisher a thumb's up. "Deal. But I'm using those bonus points to buy you a break. I can handle the kitchen for a solid fifteen minutes so you can sit down."

Fisher smiles at me. "How'd I get so lucky?"

I push open the swinging doors and enter the dining room with my chin raised. I'm normally not a confrontational girl, but cross Marianne, and I go for the throat.

Despite the fact that Jeremy is signing an autograph for someone, I plop myself down in the chair across from him at his table for two. "Well, if it isn't Jeremy Johnson."

Jeremy turns his focus to me, a vague recognition

coming over his face. "Ah. You're the receptionist at the lawyer's office." Then his face falls when he realizes I know all about the skeletons in his closet (or more accurately, in the backseat of the car he drove into town).

"Charlotte," I tell him, motioning to myself.

Jeremy nods, his complexion sallow. "Nice to see you again. I didn't realize you lived in Sweetwater Falls."

Once the person who asked for the autograph returns to her table, I fix him with an authoritative stare. "I live here and just so happen to be Marianne Magnolian's best friend."

Jeremy grimaces. "Then you know…"

I draw myself up, letting him know that I am not a person to lie to. "I know all about what you've done. In fact, I was at the Colonel's General Store a few days ago and saw you there."

"Oh. I didn't see you." He sips his water, giving me a glimpse of his black and gray teeth.

Well done, Fisher.

I cross my arms. "I figured. Otherwise, you might have kept your little phone call private from my ears."

After he puts the pieces together, his eyes widen. "What? I'm not sure what you heard, but there's a perfectly good explanation why I was talking to her."

I lean forward, my jaw firm with displeasure. "I don't care about your reasons. I want you to come clean and stop this cheating behavior you seem to think is okay. You're not doing this again. Not in my town."

It's then that it occurs to me that, even though I didn't grow up here, Sweetwater Falls is my town. I belong here. I know who wears the mascot costumes to all the festivals. I know who is favored to win at the poker tournament the Live Forever Club is holding next week. I know when the mail is delivered.

I know that the Head Librarian deserves better than half a man's heart.

Jeremy shoots me a look laced with guilt and exhaustion. "Look, I've been up most of the night barfing up bad fish. I'm not best self right now, but I hear you. I'll keep my phone calls more private."

"Wrong answer." I press my pointer finger to the tabletop. "You'll leave her alone. She deserves better than to be caught up in the mess you've created for yourself. And you'll also start talking to cops who are not Logan. He isn't at your beck and call. If your story is worth hearing, then any police officer is qualified to hear it."

Jeremy narrows his eyes at me, sizing me up. "What do you care about Logan? I thought this was a female solidarity thing."

I lean back in my seat, one leg crossed over the other. "Logan is my boyfriend, and you've put him in an awkward situation that doesn't make him look all that great to his colleagues."

"How's that?"

"You aren't coming clean about the whole story. If Logan doesn't solve this murder, and he is the only one you'll talk to, then the blame is going to fall on him the longer this gets dragged out." I motion to Jeremy. "If you know more about the murder, then say so. Tell Logan today. Now, in fact." I fix Jeremy with an expectant expression. "Right now."

Jeremy glowers at me, though the conviction is weak. "Oh, fine. It's not like I was purposefully withholding information from Logan. I just didn't want to point the finger at someone who is most likely innocent. But fine. If you need me to tell him everything, I will. Just stop looking at me like that."

"Like what? Like I expect more from someone Marianne used to hold in high esteem? Like I expect you to be a decent human being who cares more about helping out than protecting yourself? If you have nothing to hide, then tell Logan what he needs to know."

Jeremy pulls his phone from his pocket, glancing around because he is very much aware that he always has an audience.

"Logan? Hey, man. I might have information that could be helpful. Or not. I don't know." He pinches the bridge of his nose. "Melanie Montagne is my girlfriend, but I've been seeing someone else on the side. Julia Green."

My spine stiffens. I expect him to mention Marianne, but he breezes right over that indiscretion.

What a weasel.

"Both girls have not been thrilled with my new

contract. It was like going from one argument to an identical one when I was with them."

My brows pinch together, since this is not where I was expecting him to go with this.

Jeremy continues, his chin low and his volume even lower. "Melanie was particularly vocal about how much of our time together would be sacrificed with this new contract. So, I started spending more time with Julia on the side."

What an absolute scumbag.

Logan must be talking, because after a few beats, Jeremy replies, "I was with Julia during the time of Ray's death, so I know Julia didn't kill Ray. I didn't want to tell you, because that would put me in some seriously hot water with Melanie, my girlfriend. But sure, you can call Julia and check my whereabouts with her. Sorry I didn't tell you sooner. You can see why I didn't mention Julia."

After a few more back and forths, Jeremy ends the call. He casts me a petulant scowl. "There. Are you happy? I just brought a woman into the mix who I don't exactly want dragged into this mess."

I lean forward with pure malice in my eyes. "You're done stringing her along. Do what you want when you're on the road, but here in Sweetwater Falls, we look after our own. You should know better than to pull that multiple girls garbage here." I stand so I can enjoy the feel of towering over him. "End it, and end it now." I pick up his glass of water before I can stop myself. I've clearly over-stepped, but this final act is my spite coming to life.

I splash his ice water in his face, garnering gasps from everyone in the dining room.

I set down the empty glass, watching the water droplets trickle over his chin and nose. I'm shocked that I did something so brazen.

I guess I really am Charlotte the Brave when my best friend's heart is at stake.

I stalk out of the dining area with my head held high, hoping this is the last I will have to see of Jeremy Johnson.

CONFRONTING MARIANNE

$\mathcal{M}$y fifth attempt at knitting is much the same as the first four: Agnes patiently walks me through the steps. I think I am doing them correctly. Then I try to do the next row, and my stitching on the row above was too tight to make another row possible. I then get frustrated and tear it all out, starting from scratch and swearing this time will be different. I will make my stitches looser and everything will fall into place.

I slam my knitting needles on the round table in Aunt Winnie's kitchen, startling all three members of the Live Forever Club. "I can't do this! I can't focus. I'm too mad. All my stitches are too tight. I don't need to make a scarf. I'll make... I'll make a yarn worm. That's what I'll make. There, it's done."

Agnes chortles at my frustration. "Oh, honey. It's alright. It takes a while to get the rhythm of it, but after you do, everything falls into place. It will come to you when you're ready for it. Until then, perhaps you should stretch or talk it out. You're so tightly wound today."

I make a show of crossing my arms over my chest like the petulant child I am. "Today and every day that Jeremy is still in Sweetwater Falls. I'm going on a double date with Carlos and Marianne tonight, and I'm worried I will shake her the second I see her. I don't know what she sees in Jeremy. He's the worst."

Karen sips her tea, then goes back to her knitting. "While I was taking care of her when she was sick, I thought for sure she would open up to me about his phone calls, but nothing. She said she didn't want to even think his name."

"Can't say I blame her there," I grumble.

Aunt Winifred holds up her work of art. "What do you think?"

I gasp at the yarn that was once wadded into a ball, and is now a beautiful blanket with a hood, so you can wear it like a cape. "That's incredible!" I stare at the blanket wistfully. "Can I tell you I wish I could knit something as cool as that?"

Aunt Winnie chuckles. "You'd better get ready, honey cake. Aren't you supposed to meet Logan soon?"

I nod just as the doorbell rings. "I guess that's my cue." I move to the door and greet Logan with a kiss to his cheek, hoping to leave my foul mood behind. "Right on time."

Logan shoves his hands in the pockets of his beige pants. "I was in my truck for like, ten minutes, actually. I didn't want to seem too eager to see you." He grimaces. "And I just ruined my cool façade by telling you that."

I snicker at his cuteness. "Your timing is perfect, and so are you. I was in a grumpy mood. I needed to vent about it before you showed up, so I didn't spew my unhappiness all over you."

Logan steps inside while I fish my coat off the rack. He helps me thread my arms through. I love the way his knuckles slip across my shoulder. "What were you upset about?" he asks me. "I'm a good listener."

"Of course you are," I say with a smirk. "You're good at everything. But I don't think worrying about Jeremy's intentions with Marianne is good date talk."

Logan's expression tightens. "I was thinking the same thing before I rang the doorbell, so don't hold back on my account. I'm glad we're going out with Marianne and Carlos, but I don't think I can make it through an entire movie without saying something."

"Me either."

"I like Carlos. If something fishy is going on, I'm not going to leave my buddy out to dry. If the shoe was on the other foot, and Carlos knew you were seeing someone else on the side, I would be frustrated if he didn't tell me straightaway." He throws his head back, exasperated with himself. "I swore I wasn't going to bring my frustration into the house, yet here I am."

Logan proffers his arm to me after we say goodbye to the Live Forever Club. He walks me to his navy pickup truck, which can handle the snow far better than my car. He opens the door for me and helps me inside, since the truck is so tall.

When he shuffles around the front of the car and then lets himself inside, he shivers in the driver's seat. "Man, it's cold." He starts up the engine and cuts me a wary side eye. "So, we're not talking about Jeremy. Is that right?"

I sigh, slumping against the seat. "You know I'm not that strong. What new drama is there, or is it more of the same?"

Logan pulls onto the street, his grassy green eyes focused on the road ahead while the snow falls. "Melanie and Jeremy are fighting, which he felt the need to go into detail about with me before giving me actual useful information on the case."

"Ugh. You're a good person. I don't think I could listen to him whine about his relationship."

Logan purses his lips before he continues. "That contract Jeremy was offered is nuts. It's got him on the road nearly every single day for two years with no increase in pay. And Ray wanted the rights to any new songs Jeremy writes on the tour. It's a bad contract, for sure. I can see why Jeremy was upset about it."

"That is crummy. I can't imagine wanting to be famous so badly that I'd give away the rights to something that's mine."

"Fame, money. I'm not sure the motivator. Doesn't really matter anymore, because now that Ray is dead, that contract is a no-go."

I click my seatbelt. "Is that good news or bad news?"

Logan shrugs. "Depends on how you look at it. Someone else from the label is going to take charge of the tour, which is good because that means the tour doesn't have to end. But a big part of why Jeremy got that gig in the first place was..." Logan shoots me a culpable look, like he doesn't want to say something bad about anyone, even Jeremy.

"What?"

Logan holds up one hand in surrender, as if to excuse his forthcoming harshness. "Jeremy told me that the main reason he got the coveted second spot on the tour instead of being the opening act was because he's dating Melanie, Ray's daughter. He was supposed to be an opening act on like, two stops along the tour. But once he started dating Melanie, he was bumped up to the number two spot, and made a permanent act."

I shake my head at the blatant display of nepotism, though I already knew as much. "You know, I keep waiting to hear something about this guy that isn't horrible, but every detail makes me dislike him more." I run my hands through my blonde curls, wishing I'd taken Agnes up on her advice to actually put two minutes into getting ready for my date. I wish I'd run a brush through my hair, at least. "I can understand why Jeremy and Melanie are at odds. She would miss him if he's on the road for two whole years."

Logan shakes his head. "That's the thing. Melanie is one of his backup singers on the tour, so if anything, she should be overjoyed. They would spend literally every single day together."

My brows furrow. "Then what were they fighting about? Does Melanie know about Marianne?"

Logan shrugs. "It didn't sound like it. But I supposed I can put that on the list of things to ask Jeremy when I see him in the afternoon tomorrow."

"Might be a good idea." I pretend to dance in my seat. "Are you ready for our double date?"

Logan chuckles, shaking his head. "Not even a little bit. I'm glad to see you, but I hate dealing with tension like what we're about to walk into. I'm no good at keeping secrets when someone could get hurt."

"Me either."

The two of us do our best to discuss the trailer for the movie we are about to see, which lasts us until we get to the movie theater.

Logan looks like he might be ill by the time we park, though I know it's not another bout of food poisoning. What's weighing him down is the burden of knowing he has to keep a secret from Carlos, with whom he is about to come face to face.

Marianne waves at us from just inside the lobby, her

beverage already in her hand. Her smile isn't as peppy as usual, but she looks happy to see us.

She kisses my cheek after we come in through the door she pops open for us. "Hey, guys. This was a good idea. I needed to get out of the house. Thanks for planning this."

The lobby of the theater has large posters lining the walls and about a dozen people milling about, waiting for their movie to start. I wave to Delia, who smiles at me beside Frank.

Glad to see they're out having fun together. I like watching people when they're happy.

Carlos trots over from the drinking fountain and hands us two tickets. "Here you are. My treat for all the help you gave me when you moved me into the new office. This is the first night I've come up for air."

"It's good to..." I start, but my words die when Logan explodes.

His eyes are wide as he points at Marianne. "Jeremy's been calling Marianne and sweettalking her!" He squinches his eyes shut and lets out a noise of frustration. "I'm sorry, Carlos. I'm sorry, Marianne. I can't keep something like that to myself. I appreciate that you're in a rough situation, what with Jeremy being back in town, but I like Carlos, and he deserves better." Logan shakes out his hands and then bends over at the waist as if he just ran a mile. "I'm sorry I'm ruining the night! You know I can't keep something like that a secret. Not if Carlos is going to get hurt."

Marianne and Carlos both stare at Logan in stunned silence, their eyes wide.

My hand clamps over my mouth because that was certainly not the plan for the night. I am torn between horror and hysterical laughter at Logan's outburst, so I remain mute and watch the mood of group shift uncertainly.

Carlos' mouth pops open. His brows furrow in confusion as he turns to his date. "Uh, Marianne?"

Marianne gapes at Logan. "Where are you getting your information from? I haven't spoken to Jeremy since the day he stopped in your office with a dead body in the backseat. He hasn't called me, and he certainly isn't sweettalking me. I can't even fathom how something like that would go."

I raise my hand sheepishly. "I heard him talking to you. Jeremy was on the phone with you while he was in the Colonel's General Store. Called you 'sugarbean'."

Marianne goes from stunned to livid. "He said *what?* That's what he used to call me."

"I know."

Marianne's glower makes her look like she could cut glass with her molten glare. "Jeremy is calling his girlfriend 'sugarbean'? That's low."

Now I am thoroughly confused. "He was talking with some woman named Julia, not wanting anyone to find out he was cheating on Melanie with her. Then he called, well, I thought he called you, because he referred to her as 'sugarbean'. He was talking sweet and saying he..." I shake my head. "I'm sure he was talking to you!"

Marianne's nose scrunches. "Well, I don't know what to tell you about that, but I'm not his sugarbean anymore. Jeremy hasn't spoken to me since that day he came back into town. More likely than not, he doesn't have the sense to come up with a new nickname for Melanie, but recycled the one he had for me." Her nose scrunches. "How lazy. I mean, that's just insulting."

My hand goes over my mouth. "This whole time, it wasn't you? You're not his sugarbean?"

Marianne's cheeks turn pink with barely controlled rage. "If Jeremy called me that now, I'm not sure I could keep my temper. Let some other woman answer to that stupid nickname. Fine by me. She can have the name, and she can have him."

Of all things, Carlos chuckles. "I was feeling insecure until the sugarbean nickname surfaced. Is it okay if I just call you 'Marianne'?"

Marianne softens by a noticeable degree. "I prefer it." Then Marianne massages her temples. "If Jeremy is cheating on his girlfriend, well, that's no real surprise. But he's not cheating with me."

I balk at the misinformation I have been operating under, assuming it all as fact. "He must have called Julia, and then called Melanie, not you. I'm so relieved! Oh, Marianne, all this time, I thought you were secretly getting back with Jeremy."

Marianne blanches. "No. No and never. If I ever entertain something like that, you have my full permission to take me to the doctor for a brain scan."

I shake my head. "And I confronted Jeremy about it at The Snuggle Inn. I threw a glass of water in his face for doing that to you."

Marianne covers her mouth, breaking into giggles. "You did what?"

I am exasperated with myself. "I didn't know he wasn't cheating with you! You deserve someone wonderful, like Carlos."

Carlos' chest puffs while Marianne coos at the notion that I would attack Jeremy for her. "That's so sweet."

"I'm glad that's where you're landing with all of this. I'm embarrassed I didn't come out and ask you days ago."

Marianne tilts her head to the side. "To be fair, my head was in the toilet for a sizeable chunk of the week. I'm not sure I would have had the brainpower to process all of it."

Logan mops the sweat off his brow with his hand. "I'm so glad that's done with. I was going out of my mind." He casts me a look of pure exhaustion at having kept the secret for so long. "If you're ever wondering if I'll be unfaithful, this is how strongly I feel about that sort of thing." His eyes lock in on mine. "I'm in this, Miss Charlotte."

My heart thumps loudly in my chest. "I'm in this, too."

It's amazing how a crush turned into affection, and

then birthed into something real. For a second, I forget all about the murder we are trying to solve so I can appreciate the man who doesn't know how to be duplicitous. I love his kind nature, and vow to do all I can to protect it, since that is a rare gift to the world, indeed.

Marianne coos again, her hand over her heart. "Well, that was worth all the misplaced drama if it led you two to that moment. I'm glad I got to witness it."

My mind returns to the matter at hand. My fingers fix to my hips. "That still doesn't get us any closer to solving the mystery of who killed Ray Montagne. I want that fake cowboy out of Sweetwater Falls as soon as possible."

Marianne nods. "Agreed. We'll figure it out, Charlotte the Brave. We always do." Then she links her arm through mine and turns us toward the theater, so that for a few hours, we can tune out the questions that plague us.

SURPRISE VISITOR

*B*aking is always a good distraction for me, but today I need it more than most. I'm not completely behind on my cupcake orders; I know I will get them all filled. But the pep in my step can be attributed to the push I feel to race against the clock. I need to make up for lost time when I had food poisoning. The fact that Logan came over to make sure I had plenty of frosting is no small blessing. I need every boost today, since my customers will start coming to the kitchen to pick up their orders momentarily.

I need to get three dozen more cupcakes frosted in the next few minutes without making them look like they were done in haste. The sun is up, which means my customers will be here soon.

I fill the piping bag with more fudge frosting, grateful

that I don't have an audience for the sweat trickling down my nape.

I've been at the Bravery Bakery kitchen since four this morning, and it's nearly nine o'clock, which is when people can start picking up their orders. My business is growing, which is a gift I cannot believe I get to experience. However, after coming off a bout of food poisoning and having my mind preoccupied with murder and trying to get Jeremy out of town as fast as possible, I'm a little behind.

I do my best to breathe steadily, calming myself as much as I am able while I pipe rosettes one at a time and then place each cupcake in the pink boxes. Even when I hear a car door slam in the parking lot, I do not rush my process. Each cupcake deserves my full attention. They are a gift to the town I love, so I will not cut corners with my gratitude.

I am halfway through the remainder of the cupcakes when a fist bangs on the door. Apparently, the sign I have hanging is not enough of a deterrent. *"Open at 9am"* seems to be pretty straightforward, but apparently someone wants their order at five minutes till.

I plaster on a polite smile as I set down my piping bag and then make my way to the door. "I'm sorry, I'm just..." I start, but when my eyes take in the cowboy hat and lanky stature of Jeremy Johnson, my jaw tightens. "We're closed."

I make to slam the door in his face, but Jeremy catches

the door and takes a step forward. "Please. I know you hate me, but I don't know where else to turn."

I balk at him. "You've got to be kidding me. You're turning to me in whatever hour of need this is? I'm the girl who threw a glass of water in your face, if you recall. I am the last person who can help you even if I wanted to, which I don't."

Jeremy shuts the heavy door behind him, making himself a fixture in my bakery, which now feels tarnished by his presence. "Hear me out, Carly. Please."

"It's Charlotte." My nostrils flare with frustration. "My gosh, do women even register as humans to you?"

"Apologies, Charlotte."

I go back to my piping bag and fix my eyes on my remaining cupcakes. While I realize I might have just allowed a murderer into my bakery, I'm too mad at him to be afraid. Granted, now that I know he isn't cheating with Marianne, my anger has dipped itself in a new color, but it's there all the same. He cheated on her after asking her to marry him. That is absolutely vulgar.

"Go away," I admonish him, piping my rosettes.

Jeremy takes off his hat and rests it over his chest as if that's some sort of gentlemanly plea. "I'd thought Logan would hear me out and understand that I'm not guilty, but that doesn't seem to be the case. I know you two are dating, so I figured maybe if I could convince you, then you could make a plea to him on my behalf."

I scoff at his farfetched idea. "I cannot imagine you

have anything to say that I would be interested in hearing." I squeeze the icing from the base of the bag toward the tip, keeping my eyes on my work as if his presence doesn't vex me or throw me off my game one bit. "You asked Marianne to marry you, and then you cheated on her. She's my best friend."

Jeremy's mouth firms. "You know, I have a side to that story, too."

"No, you don't," I snap at him. "You don't get a side. She's my best friend. Clearly you don't understand how friendships work. She cries, and you go down in history as scum. End of story."

Jeremy sighs. "Fine. I'm scum. I cheated on a sweet girl. But that's not what I came here to talk about."

The fact that he has hat hair makes me devilishly glad. I hope he has a stain on his shirt, too. I hope he scuffs his shiny cowboy boots.

I have five cupcakes left, and I refuse to finish late. "Talk away, then. Whatever gets you out of here quicker. If Logan isn't convinced by your lies, I can't imagine I'll be the one who will be persuaded you're a terrific guy who was just in the wrong place at the wrong time."

Jeremy's volume climbs. "I will not go to jail for a crime I didn't commit!"

I pause as my conscience taps me on the shoulder. Though I would very much like to see Jeremy behind bars, if he didn't kill Ray, then Ray Montagne's killer is still out there, and will likely strike again.

I sigh, already prepared to dismiss whatever comes out of Jeremy's mouth next. "Alright. Talk."

Jeremy pulls out my stool as if he owns the place and plops down atop it. He sags on the seat, as if he is the one who has been on his feet since four in the morning.

I cannot stand this guy.

Jeremy sets his cowboy hat on his knee. "I didn't kill Ray. We had an argument, and it was pretty public. I mean, not for the fans to hear, but everyone on the tour who was within shouting distance heard me giving Ray a piece of my mind."

"Charming," I offer, my sass in full swing. I have one cupcake left, thank goodness. One cupcake and one minute left before nine o'clock. I will not allow myself to drop the ball on my dream job. I won't be a business who does not do what it promises. If I say the cupcakes will be ready at nine in the morning, then by golly, I will make good on my word.

Jeremy runs his hand over his jaw. It's then I realize he hasn't shaved. He has bags under his eyes and actually looks troubled.

Good. That's what murderers should feel.

Jeremy's shoulders lower. "The contract was awful. Effectively doubled the days I would be on the clock without a penny of a raise."

I blanche at the notion. "That sounds like something you shouldn't sign."

"I didn't. I took it back to the tour bus to mull it over. I mean, the industry—at least from where I stand—will spit you out if you don't take the offer they give you, no matter how insulting. I knew that if I didn't sign, Ray would replace me on the tour."

I am torn between wanting to blow off his pain and offering up some sympathy. So I split the different and say nothing as I package up my last order just in time.

A knock bangs on the door. "Excuse me. And stay out of sight. I don't want people to know you're in here. I don't want anyone to think that we're friends."

Jeremy chuckles sadly. "Fine, fine." He moseys to the far side of the kitchen when I open the door.

"Hi, Marcus. I have a dozen cupcakes ready for your movie night. How's your dog?"

Marcus grins at me. "Doing well. He's going on a walk with Beanie this afternoon."

I grin at him. "Tell Beanie's mom I said she's got a sweet boyfriend. I put extra double fudge in your order, since those are Lisa's favorite."

Marcus takes the box from me with a smile. "Thanks. Double fudge scores me double the brownie points."

After Marcus exits, my smile fades. I move back to the counter and start arranging my boxes by alphabetical order, using the first name of the person who will be picking them up.

Jeremy leans against the far wall, his boot kicked back against it and his hands crossed over his chest. "I didn't realize you were capable of being nice."

"Well, Marcus didn't murder anyone, so he gets extra double fudge," I simper, my attitude in full swing.

"And I get the Frost Queen because I'm a big, bad murderer?"

"That's how it works."

Jeremy sighs. "Only I didn't murder anyone. Though, I did cheat on Marianne, so I suppose the Frost Queen isn't thawing anytime soon."

"It's a hard permafrost. And do you have a point? The sooner you make it, the sooner you can leave. We were at the part where you're a poor, sad musician sitting in your tour bus with a bad contract."

"So you were listening. That plays in my favor."

"I might stop listening soon, so get on with it."

Jeremy studies my movements while I alphabetize. "I can help, you know. Put me to work."

I hope the look I cast him tells him just how much I would appreciate his help with anything.

Jeremy backs off, holding up his hands and returning to the topic. "I couldn't sign the contract. Even after talking it over with Melanie, my girlfriend, I couldn't do it. She was all excited because it would mean we would be together every single day for two years. I had... mixed feelings about that."

I don't want to hear about his feelings. Nothing that humanizes him is a good conversation in my book.

Jeremy keeps going, as if I have asked for more details. "You're not going to like this next part."

I snort at his warning. "I can imagine."

"I didn't want to be on the road every single day because my girlfriend is one of my backup singers. Ray's daughter Melanie was a big part of why I got such a sweet spot on the tour this early in my career. But working side by side with her every single day? It's not how I do relationships."

I mime gagging in his direction. Honestly, I don't know what kind of an audience he thought I would be for this conversation. I feel no need to feign maturity.

"I didn't kill Ray because after I got the contract, I went away for a night. The tour was stopped, and I'd done all my press appearances. I wanted some time to myself. So I rented a hotel room to clear my head. I was in that hotel room when Ray was killed."

It's not exactly the perfect exoneration, but it's a factor to consider. "I don't suppose anyone can corroborate your story, can they?"

Jeremy studies the toe of his boot. "That's the thing. Someone can corroborate my story, but that would be a bit of a problem for me. See, I wasn't in the hotel room by myself."

I shoot him a look of sheer exasperation. Though I knew as much, hearing him admit to being a cheating jerk revs up my frustration afresh.

I want him to say the words. I want him to admit full stop that he cheated, and he is scum.

I scowl at the man. "You said you wanted to get away to

clear your head and do some thinking. If you went with Melanie, just tell Logan. He can corroborate your story and take you off the list of suspects. I don't know why you need to be here, talking to me."

Jeremy bites down on his lower lip and shoves his hands in the pockets of his jeans. "See, that's the thing. I wasn't with Melanie." He pauses for so long; I think he is waiting for me to ask him who he was with. He keeps his eyes from me when he finally speaks. "There's this other woman I've been spending time with. I went to the hotel to blow off some steam, and later that night, a woman I've been seeing on the side met up with me."

If I have known a man worse than Jeremy, I cannot recall him now. I count my lucky stars that Marianne is not dating this man.

13

JEREMY'S LIE AND ALIBI

I don't know what to say when Jeremy confesses that he has fashioned himself yet another love triangle with which to hang himself. "You're telling me that you couldn't have killed Ray, because at the time of his death, you were cheating on your girlfriend—Ray's daughter—with another woman?"

"Julia got there around midnight, but I was checked in by myself at the hotel before that during the day. It's a pretty solid alibi, but I can't use it. You understand."

My tone rises to a shrill note. "No, I don't! I will never understand that sort of behavior! Why would you think I might understand?"

Jeremy kicks his foot off the wall, taking a step toward me. "You understand that I can't tell Logan who my alibi is. He'll have to question her. That information goes into the report. Do you think journalists can't get their hands on those reports? I'll be ruined!"

I guffaw at him. "How big is your ego that you think people care that much about your horrible attempt at a love life?"

Jeremy runs his hands through his hair. "I make my living off of writing love ballads. My brand is that I am a faithful, lovesick man with a muse. Everyone knows that my muse is my backup singer. If it gets out that I cheated on Melanie? Forget the tour. None of my fanbase is going to listen to another love song I write, because they'll all think they're not genuine."

"But they're not genuine! You're cheating on Melanie! You're stepping out on your muse."

Jeremy throws his head back. "This is about more than just relational logistics, Charlotte. I will lose my career if this gets out."

I pinch the bridge of my nose, trying to keep up. "So let me get this straight. You're willing to go to jail to save your crooner reputation? How much better a record deal do you think a murder rep will get you?"

Jeremy rubs the nape of his neck. "I was hoping the police would have found the actual killer by now. I don't want to have that information out there. I don't want to break Melanie's heart. I can't have her finding out about Julia. She won't handle that well."

I raise an eyebrow at him. "How exactly does a person

handle it well when they're being cheated on? How did you expect this would play out?"

Jeremy takes a long inhale before he answers. "Melanie is prone to theatrics. She's a bit of a diva. Like, stopped a song in the middle of a performance because the band came in a beat early. If Ray wasn't her father, she would have been fired a long time ago."

I scoff at him. "I love that you cheat on Melanie, yet you have the gall to try and make her sound like the unreasonable one. I can't even with you."

"I didn't mean to hurt anyone."

I cross my arms over my chest. "Yes, you did. When you cheat on someone, you are not trying to be kind to them."

Jeremy shakes his head at me, as if I am being unreasonable. "Believe what you want, but I care about Melanie. I didn't mean to do this to her. I don't want her finding out about Julia."

I keep my voice as steady as I am able. "Did you mean to murder Ray?"

Jeremy throws up his hands. "I didn't murder Ray! I have the credit card receipt to prove I was at the hotel with Julia that night. We even got a late checkout, so I was nowhere near the scene of the crime. I came back to the tour bus, lived my life and didn't see Ray that whole day. Then the next morning, Ray didn't wake me up like he usually does. I went out and found Ray in his car, dead, when I went to confront him about the contract. Judging by the smell, he died well before I found him, which means I have an alibi that puts me far from the scene of his murder when it took place."

I turn back to my pink boxes of cupcakes, doing my best to put them in proper order. "Then how did your contract get into Ray's mouth? If you wanted to do some thinking, then why didn't you have the contract with you?"

Jeremy shakes his head. "I couldn't find it. After Melanie and I had an argument about it, I went to the tour bus and packed a bag for the hotel. I thought I had it with me, but I didn't." He shrugs. "That one's a mystery to me."

These are not the kinds of conversations I envisioned when I set up the Bravery Bakery here. I want to be talking about frosting and cupcake flavors. I want to sing songs about sprinkles, not have glib back and forths about crime scenes.

"And you were arguing with Melanie about..."

Jeremy moves over to the counter a few feet away from me. "Melanie thought the contract was great. She didn't understand why I didn't want to sign it. When I explained that it basically made me a prisoner with no time off for good behavior, she took that to mean I thought our relationship was like a prison." Then Jeremy mutters, "Which, I mean, isn't too far a stretch."

My upper lip curls with indignation. "Don't tell me how terrible she is. If you want to break up with her, do it. No one is forcing you to be with her. It's slimy not to end things, but sneak off with someone else when you're unhappy."

Jeremy peeks into one of the boxes, so I slap his hand. He casts me an apologetic look. "I can't exactly dump a woman whose father was just murdered. That seems kind of low."

"Lower than cheating on her while her father was being murdered? Because you're not exactly aiming for the moral high ground, here." I pause as something else dawns on me. "Your nickname for Melanie. What is it? Sweetheart? Honey bunches?"

Jeremy's neck shrinks. "'Sugarbean'. That's my name for her."

"You were talking to Melanie on the phone in the Colonel's General Store. I overheard you. That was your cutesy name for Marianne, you realize. You've got to know that's rude—recycling girlfriend nicknames like that."

"I'm getting quite the education today." Jeremy lowers his head. "This whole scenario is not my finest moment. I'm hanging on by a thread, here, Charlotte. I don't know how to juggle it all. I need you to talk to Logan for me."

I glower at him. "You realize this is a problem you created, right? You are entirely responsible for your own misery."

Jeremy presses his palms together, pleading for me to understand. "Please, Charlotte. Talk to Logan. Tell him I'm innocent. I can't go on the record with my alibi, but if you tell him, he won't have to put it in his report that I was with Julia at the time of Ray's murder. I didn't kill my manager!"

When a knock sounds on the back door, I am grateful for the interruption.

As much as I want Jeremy locked up and the key thrown away, I can't shake the feeling that he is telling me the truth. His story is grim and embarrassing, for certain, but that's why I believe it. If his alibi had him off doing something altruistic, I would not give a second of credence to the lie.

I hand off the cupcakes to the next person and the next, all the while pondering who could have murdered Ray, and whether or not Jeremy will ever grow up.

14

KNITTING AND CROSS STITCHING

*I*f I never try knitting again, that will be fine.

Agnes, however, is determined I will not give up her favorite pastime. "Loose stitching, dear. You're going to have to tear those out and start over again."

I throw my head back because I cannot focus on this task when my mind is otherwise occupied. I hand my knitting needles and the one useable row of stitching to Marianne.

My best friend finally agreed to come over instead of cooping herself up in her house yet again. It's good to see her sitting on Aunt Winnie's mauve couch, like it's any old normal day.

"You fix it," I whine to her.

Marianne scoffs. "I don't know why you think I would be able to get this any better than you can. I won't even try knitting. Kudos to you for battling the yarn." She holds up her wooden hoop with canvas stretched across the frame. "Needlepoint is my mountain to climb. Knitting is yours."

"I picked the wrong mountain," I complain as I tear out the row of stitches I did too tightly.

Again.

"Me, too." Marianne holds up her needlepoint, which has the wrong color for the sunset, and several of the X stitches misshapen.

Agnes takes a sip of her tea. "After you get the hang of your projects, this will be a time of relaxation for you both. You'll be able to sit down and watch a movie while making something beautiful. It's quite rewarding."

I motion to Agnes' pile of perfectly knitted triangles. "That's because you're good at it. In the time I have taken to make this one row seven times the wrong way, you have made eight triangles."

"Ten," Agnes corrects me. "And I've been knitting longer than you've been alive, so it's hardly a fair comparison. You have to walk before you can run. You'll get there."

I hold up my disaster of a project. "Before or after I run myself through with one of these needles?"

Agnes keeps her eyes on her triangle. "Preferably before."

"I give up. Let's switch," Marianne suggests, handing me her needlepoint. "I can't look at this thing anymore. I'd rather fail at knitting than fail at cross stitch over and over again."

I grimace, fairly certain that I will not be any more

successful at needlepoint than I am at knitting. However, I take the wooden hoop and needle from Marianne, recalling the many tips Agnes bestowed upon Marianne during our crafting session.

I take a deep breath while I discreetly undo a few misshapen stitches so I can start fresh. I'm not sure I can do a better job of bringing this Sweetwater Falls sunset to life, but at this point, I will do anything to keep from having to pick up those knitting needles again.

Marianne, it seems, has no trouble putting the many lessons Agnes has given me and applying them with only a few tips from Agnes to get her going.

Marianne is a natural at knitting, it seems. She concocts a whole row that is loose and useable by the time I finish undoing her unruly stitches, so I can start with a blank slate on my fabric.

I take another deep breath before I begin, because I remember Agnes, Karen and Aunt Winnie saying this was supposed to be a way to relax. But after the morning I've had, I am not sure anything can undo the knots in my shoulders.

Still, I give needlepointing a go, hoping it distracts me as much as soothes me.

Agnes keeps her eyes on the multi-colored triangle that is dangling from her knitting needles. "You know, I heard a funny story this afternoon when Karen and I were helping to set up for the Knit Your Heart Out fair."

Marianne is already looping into the next row. She makes it look so easy. "What's that?"

Agnes keeps her tone light and her gaze from us. "Oh, just that Jeremy stopped by the Bravery Bakery this morning. Laura told Sally, who told Delia that he was in the kitchen." Her eyes flick to me. "Anything you want to talk about?"

A defeated groan escapes my lips. "Yes, but also no. I don't even like saying his name in this town, so no. But I really don't like keeping anything from Marianne, so yes. But then I know that talking about him hurts you, Marianne, so also no."

Marianne surprises me with a snicker. "That's quite the head-spin you've got going on there. Out with it. You'll feel better once it's out of your brain."

"I sincerely doubt that." I lower my nose closer to the thread as I start weaving a light blue floss through the fabric. "Jeremy came by the bakery this morning to ask me to convince Logan to not write something in his report, but to also hear the thing that would exonerate him. I think you can imagine how well that conversation went."

"Paint me a picture," Marianne requests as she knits with ease.

I swallow hard and tell them the story, not leaving out any details because I don't know which are lies and which are not.

When I finish, Marianne sets down her knitting

needles. "Are you serious? Jeremy is cheating again? What is wrong with him?"

"I'll start up a list," I grumble.

Agnes smiles at us, her round cheeks lifting. "Don't you see what good news this is? Marianne, now there is absolutely no doubt that your engagement didn't end because of anything you did. I know you've blamed yourself over the past couple years. But it had little to do with you, honey. Your relationship ended because of Jeremy's proclivities that he still hasn't managed to master."

Marianne gapes at Agnes. "I guess I never thought of it that way. I assumed I was boring. Too small for his big dreams."

Agnes dips her head. "I know, dear. But you see? Nothing could be further from the truth."

Righteous indignation boils up in me. "That's the story you've been telling yourself? Marianne, you are in charge of whole worlds. You run the library, which is where the past and the present shake hands. All languages gather under one roof—the roof you had repaired so imaginations would have a safe place to wander." I shake my head at her faulty logic. "You are not small. Your heart is big. It's Jeremy's love that was too small for this town."

Agnes nods once, her chin firm. "You are Marianne the Wild."

The declaration rings through the living room, sending a chill down my spine.

Agnes turns her head to me. "And what is your name?"

"Charlotte the Brave?" My reply sounds more like a question than an actual title I own.

Agnes motions to my purse. "Then let's see you make that phone call. Be brave, Charlotte. Be brave where Jeremy is afraid. He doesn't want to face his actions. The real killer deserves to serve time for what they did to Mister Montagne." She leans toward me as if delivering a secret. "I know you're afraid to stick your nose in the thick of it. You're afraid of Marianne getting hurt all over again. But sometimes the only way to get through something is to go through it. Let Marianne face her demons. Don't rob her of the chance to outgrow him."

I chew on my lower lip, contemplating Agnes' wisdom, which is never in short supply.

I have been overprotective of Marianne, which doesn't speak of bravery, but of fear. There is being a shield, and then there is treating a grown woman like she is incapable of hearing a foul phrase.

If Marianne is wild, then I need to be brave.

I set down my needlepoint to grab my phone, but as soon as the call connects to Logan, I pick my project back up, surprised how focused the threading keeps me, when usually my stomach would be in knots.

"Hello, Miss Charlotte," Logan answers while Agnes and Marianne give me bolstering nods. Agnes gives me a thumbs up, while Marianne tightens her fist and raises it, reminding me to be brave.

I hate that I am going to bat for Jeremy to prove his

innocence, yet I know it is the right thing to do, if we want the true murderer to go to jail.

I clear my throat, holding the hoop and the needle while I thread the light blue floss in and out of the fabric. "Logan, Jeremy isn't the killer, but I have a clue as to who is."

I didn't want to follow the trail to where it leads, because Jeremy's breadcrumbs are scattered with lies.

Once I tell Logan all that Jeremy divulged to me, I veer off into the place I have been avoiding.

Jeremy told me who the killer wasn't, but there is a clear guess as to who the killer might be.

"Logan, if Jeremy didn't murder Ray Montagne, then maybe Julia did. She couldn't have been happy that Jeremy was offered a contract that ensured he would be spending every single day for the next two years with his girlfriend. That wouldn't leave much time for her. Jeremy mentioned she met him at his hotel room later that night, which means she might have had plenty of time to do the terrible deed and then swing by the hotel for a night with Jeremy."

Logan's voice is grim. "That's a solid possibility. I'll talk to Jeremy and confirm all of this, then I'll bring her in."

I lean back in the couch, burrowing in the cushions. "I hate this whole thing. Is Jeremy always this much work?"

Logan chuckles. "This and more. You should have seen him when we would go fishing. Had to have the perfect outfit. Complained if any part of it got wet or dirty." Then

Logan changes his tune. "I'm a jerk. He's an old friend. Now I can't quite remember why."

"Two kids living in the same small town?" I guess.

"That's probably it. I'm not sure I would make those same choices, given the chance to go back."

"That's fair. You're not who you were when you were young."

"Shame that Jeremy is."

It's strange to think that who we were as children isn't who we will be forever.

After we end our phone call, I ponder how odd it is that a year ago, I was chopping salad ingredients, working at a restaurant that fed people, but left my soul starving. I was too meek, my voice too quiet to ask for what I really wanted out of life, so the world kept on moving without making space for my dreams.

I'm not that girl anymore.

I am Charlotte the Brave.

And I can needlepoint, doggone it.

Marianne snuggles in closer to my side while she knits. "You did the right thing. I know it feels crummy to let Jeremy off on such a gross technicality, but the point of it all is to catch the killer, so they don't strike again."

I lean my head to hers while I keep my eyes on the floss. "Is that the point? I thought the goal was to make sure you had a happily ever after where Jeremy is held accountable for his crappy personality."

Marianne's needles click together in a rhythm I could

never achieve. "Nah. My happily ever after has nothing to do with him."

It's such an adult thing to say. I love that Marianne has her head on her shoulders. Now she can point me in the right direction when I go off on a tangent that doesn't serve the greater good.

Maybe Jeremy thought there were better women out there than Marianne, but I am glad to say that he could not be more wrong about that.

15

OUT OF TOWN GUEST

*I*f there was ever a day I wish I had a reason to be in the precinct with Logan and the rest of the officers, it is today. Just like Jeremy, Julia will only talk to Logan, though the two have no real connection. Jeremy must have told Julia that Logan is the person to talk to, because she is due at the precinct in half an hour.

I make my way to the newsstand in town, my hands in my jacket pockets as the snow flutters to the ground. There is about two inches accumulated there, dusting everything from the street to the mailboxes.

Even though the Nosy Newsy isn't open during the snowy months, Frank is still outside at his bodega. Instead of selling magazines, newspapers and the like, anything the weather might ruin is not on display. That section has been taken over by a hot beverage stand.

The smell of the crisp, clean snow pairs well with hot

apple cider, so I buy a cup to keep something steamy in my hands.

"Good morning, New Girl," Frank greets me.

I shoot him a narrowed eye. "You know, I've lived in Sweetwater Falls for months. I'm hardly the new girl anymore."

Frank bats away my correction. "You're going to be the new girl until someone else moves to town. Then she'll be the new-new girl, and you'll be Charlotte, Winifred's niece."

I chuckle at him and shuffle in my snow boots to the basket on his bodega that usually would have a few clusters of flowers. Now that winter is in full swing, the purple flowers are fake, but no less cheery. Though I plan on seeing Logan tomorrow at the Knit Your Heart Out fair, it's our game to leave a note for each other, hidden beneath the petals in plain sight. I love the romance of it all. I look forward to Logan's notes that are equal parts friendly and flirty.

I slip my note into the basket and fish around until my fingers land on an envelope from Logan. My smile cannot be helped as I slide his letter into my pocket.

"You two are cute; you know that?" Frank's grin reveals a missing tooth. His greasy black hair is tucked underneath a knitted winter cap, his fingers tucked inside matching gloves. "Are you two lovebirds going to the Knit Your Heart Out fair?"

"We are. I've been saving up so I can really go nuts.

Next year, I want to be able to sell something of my own at the fair."

Frank shoots me a look that tells me he is impressed. "Good for you. I didn't realize you knitted."

"I don't, but I'm a crack shot at needlepoint, apparently. I'm working on a sunset scene that I'm going to make into a pillow."

It's a small thing, but I'm so proud of myself. I didn't think I would take to needlepointing, but when I couldn't sleep last night, thinking about Jeremy's mistress coming to town, I kept my mind occupied with needlepointing.

I know exactly one stitch, but it seems to work for me, especially when I have too much on my mind.

Frank shoves his hands in the pockets of his thick, brown jacket. "Maybe I'll see you there. I asked Delia to go with me, and she said yes."

I grin at him. Though Delia is a polarizing presence at times, being that she is the town gossip, I like seeing Frank go after what he wants and get it. "That's wonderful. I..."

But before I can finish my sentence, a woman I don't recognize walks by. Her high heels mark her as an out-of-towner, which isn't anything to take note of, really. But she's wearing an "American Pumpernickel Tour" jacket, which trains my eyes her way. "I've got to run, Frank. See you tomorrow night."

I'm gone before he works out his reply. My feet carry me into Bill's Diner on the heels of the woman I am positive is Jeremy's mistress, since that is who Logan is supposed to be interviewing today.

Though, I don't exactly know how to ask her anything, since I am a perfect stranger to her. But the second I walk into the Bill's Diner, I am distracted by how busy the place is. Every table is packed, and Becca appears to be the only waitress on the clock.

Without thinking anything through, I remove my jacket and hang it behind the counter. "Mind if I take that section? I've got a few minutes to kill if you need the help."

Becca sets down her tray and hugs me. "Thank you! Yes, please. If I don't take a break, I'm going to throttle someone." She turns and aims her glare in the direction of a booth by the window. "*That* someone."

Of course it's Jeremy. Why wouldn't the troublesome customer be Jeremy?

"What's he done now?" I ask as I tie a spare black apron around my waist. The woman I was following harrumphs into the booth with him, fixing him with a hurt expression.

Becca looks on the verge of tears. "He sits there for an hour nearly every morning. He orders stuff that's not on the menu and tries to pay with an autograph. Good luck getting a tip from that table. I liked it better when the restaurant cleared out when he came in. Now they swarm." She rolls her eyes. "Out of towners are the worst, am I right?"

I squeeze Becca's hand. "Go take a break. I've got this."

Not a person here looks like they are from Sweetwater Falls. It seems that when word got out that Jeremy was staying in our sweet little town, every person in the neighboring cities decided the hottest spot in town is Bill's Diner.

Or wherever Jeremy happens to be at the moment.

Bill's got to be loving this. The only time I see him smiling is when business is booming.

I make my way to the nearest table, checking on them to see how I can be helpful.

"We want what Jeremy Johnson is ordering, so wait to put our order in until he picks something."

"O-kay," I say, drawing out the response into two syllables. The next four tables say the exact same thing, so I beeline to the table in question, fixing Jeremy with a withering stare. "What can I get you two?"

Jeremy sighs and then puts down the menu. "I didn't know you worked here. I thought you were a baker."

"I am. I'm helping out for a little bit here today, though. You're in luck."

Jeremy mumbles something disparaging that I cannot make out above the din. He looks up at me, fixing me with a passive smile. "You know what I feel like today?"

My upper lip curls. "It had better be something on the menu. I'll save you the trouble. You're getting the broccoli cheese soup. It's terrible. You'll hate it."

Jeremy grimaces. "I can't eat Bill's broccoli cheese soup.

Has he changed the recipe since I moved out of Sweet-water Falls?"

"Nope. But that's all I'm bringing you." I turn to the woman, who looks irate, though not with me. "What can I get you?"

"Nothing. I'm not staying. I wouldn't want to eat with a man who accused me of being a murderer after I slept with him."

Yep, it's Julia, alright.

I tuck my order pad into my apron. "Julia, right? I'm sorry this is all going south for you. I'm sure if you just tell the police where you were at during the time of the murder, you'll never have to look at Jeremy's face again."

Most likely because you'll be in jail.

She throws her bejeweled hands in the air. "I was at practice, where Jeremy was supposed to be! I have about a dozen witnesses, too. I told Jeremy I could meet him at the hotel later that night, but he insisted on getting to the room at three. He skipped out on the soundcheck and left everyone in a bad mood. I didn't murder Ray. Why would I murder the man who signs my paychecks?"

My hip cocks to the side. "I mean, just spit-balling here, but maybe you wanted to frame Jeremy, since he won't leave his girlfriend for you."

Julia gapes up at me. "You severely overestimate how attached to our fling I am. Why do you think I wanted to get together *away* from everyone else?"

Jeremy balks at her. "You're ashamed to be with me?"

She flips her brown curls over her shoulder. "You're on your way out of the business. You have a girlfriend who would scratch my eyes out if she found out about us, yet here you are, blabbing to the police that I was with you all night long. Worst fling ever. My alibi won't do a thing for you, Jeremy, because I was at soundcheck during the time of Ray's death. You, on the other hand, claim to be alone in a hotel room, waiting for me, who cannot corroborate your story."

Jeremy's mouth tightens. "But you know that's where I was! I wouldn't lie about that!"

Julia holds up her hands. "I only know what I know. I know I didn't kill Ray, and I've got several dozen witnesses to confirm that."

Even my pursed lips can't hide my grin. Listening to Jeremy be put in his place is a joy I am grateful I get to witness. "Nothing for you, then?"

She scoffs. "Nothing for me. I'm happy to get out of this small town as soon as my name is cleared, which apparently couldn't happen over the phone."

Jeremy's volume climbs. "I didn't kill Ray! Someone has to believe me!"

I rest my clipboard on my hip, ignoring the table to my left trying to flag me down. "If it's not Julia, and if we're going to go out on a limb and trust it's not you, Jeremy (which is a big leap), then who else could have killed Ray? Is there anyone on the tour who had it out for him? You're still the most likely candidate, Jeremy."

Julia blinks at me, sizing up my question as well as me. "I mean, do I think Jeremy killed Ray? No. That list of suspects could be long. We all don't exactly love Ray. His contracts are terrible, and he always gives his daughter whatever she wants, whether or not Princess Melanie deserves it. But he signs the paychecks, so no one would actually do anything about it. I don't tour with murderers." Then, as if she has dismissed me so I no longer exist, she leans forward toward Jeremy. "Melanie has been telling anyone who will listen that you're not answering her calls anymore."

Jeremy rubs the nape of his neck. "I might have let my phone go to voicemail for a few days."

I scoff at him. "Her father just died."

Julia considers the situation for a few beats before she speaks. "If you're leaving her for me, don't bother. I'm out. We're done. You used me as your alibi, but then made me a suspect. You know I didn't kill Ray."

Jeremy's neck shrinks. "I didn't think you did. But I had to tell Logan something."

Julia stands in her seat and reaches across the booth to swat him repeatedly over the head with her purse. "You are the worst person I have ever met! You and Melanie deserve each other."

Maybe I could intervene, and get her to stop slapping him, but the entertainment is too good.

When Julia calms down and resumes her seat, I try to

stem my laughter. "I take it you don't like Melanie?" I ask, covering my giggle with my hand.

Julia's upper lip curls. "No one does. What she wants, she whines until her father gives it to her. She wanted to spend every single day with Jeremy on the tour, so Ray made it happen."

"So that's how that bad contract came about." I turn to Jeremy, who very much looks the part of the scolded puppy. "But you didn't sign the contract. I wonder how Melanie reacted to that."

Jeremy rests his elbows on the table. "Melanie was mad. That's what we fought about before I left for the hotel. She wanted me to sign the contract, so we could be together every single day for two years, and I didn't want to." He motions between Julia and himself. "It's a good thing she never found out about us."

Julia shrinks back in her seat. "I think she might suspect us, Jeremy." She points to herself. "The makeup artist and the musician? It's not all that hard to imagine."

Jeremy's eyes widen. "No, Melanie doesn't suspect a thing."

Julia nods. "The day I was meeting you at the hotel, I ran into her at practice. She asked me what I was up to later that night, and I told her I was going to Jacksonville. She got this strange look on her face. I'm telling you; she knows. She left soundcheck after I mentioned where I was headed."

I hold up my hand. "Wait, so Melanie's whereabouts were unaccounted for during the time of Ray's death, too?"

Jeremy pales, ignoring my input. "You told Melanie you were going to Jacksonville? Melanie knew that's where I was going! I told her I was getting a hotel there for the night to get some peace and quiet and really think about signing the contract." He throws his hands up in exasperation. "I can't believe you told her that!"

Julia shrugs. "What's done is done. I didn't mean to tell her anything that could link us together. Believe me, I don't want it getting out that we hooked up."

Jeremy's offense is worth another giggle.

I walk away and put in an order for broccoli and cheese soup for nearly every table in the place.

That'll make Bill's day. He loves that stuff. No matter that the cheese tastes like burnt rubber, and the broccoli is barely a sprinkling.

When Becca returns from her much-needed break, I hang up my black apron and give her a high-five before I leave.

There is one more person that needs to be on Logan's list of suspects, and I know just who it is.

RIP AND A RING

*T*hat night, Logan and I do our best not to make the evening all about the unsolved murder, though it's not exactly easy.

Rip, the Town Selectman, points to a spot a few feet from where I stand as I hold onto the side of the folding table. "Move that table a little to the left. That's right. No, left, not right. Good."

Logan and I look comical, I'm sure, scooting the table this way and that to accommodate Rip's particular aesthetic that only he can envision.

Setting up for the Knit Your Heart Out fair was supposed to be a two-hour commitment. At least, that's how Karen sold me on it. But we're four hours into the job and we're still not finished. My date with Logan has been surrendered to helping about a dozen people set up for the fair.

"You're a good guy to help out," I say to Logan. "You didn't even sign up, yet here you are."

Logan stretches out his shoulder. "Well, you didn't give me much of a choice when you said you would have to cancel our date because you would be helping Rip here." He motions around the spacious high school gym.

I look around at all the work we've done so far, arms akimbo. "I can't believe how much we've transformed the place." I motion to the far wall. "Hanging that huge black curtain over the closed-down bleachers really makes a difference. It was quite the eyesore before that."

Logan scoots his end of the table forward an inch so it's perfectly on the sideline of the basketball court. "That's Rip's thing with events. He wants to make sure it's an experience, not just a thing to do."

"I love that. I hope you know how lucky you are, growing up here."

Logan nods. "I can't imagine living anywhere else. Whenever someone moves out of town, I always wonder why. Maybe big towns are nice, but I like the pace of life here." His expression hardens as he stares ahead at nothing in particular.

I migrate to his side, bumping his hip with mine. "Whatcha thinking about?"

Logan breaks out of his momentary funk, his shoulders softening as he turns his chin toward my face. "Not what I should be thinking about. I'm no fun tonight. When a case is still open, I have a hard time thinking about anything else. You dream in cupcakes? I dream in puzzles, and Ray Montagne's puzzle is missing one very important piece—a plausible killer."

I stick close to his side, taking a breather from helping Rip. "I like that you care about justice for people you don't even know. It's a wonderful quality."

The corner of Logan's mouth crooks. "Is it a habit of yours to see the good in everybody?"

I tug the sleeves of the lavender cardigan that Agnes made me over my hands so I can fiddle with the edges. "I wish I could say that was true, but I can't think of a single redeeming quality about Jeremy."

"You're not alone in that. How a guy like that managed to rope in two women is beyond me."

I nod to Rip, who motions for us to grab one of the tablecloths and drape it over our table. "I'm glad Marianne isn't one of those two women. At least there's that."

"Agreed."

I move to the bin of black tablecloths and pull one out. I feel like a fancy waiter at a fine dining establishment, fanning out the cloth over the long table. I can only imagine what sorts of colorful knitted things will be displayed here for sale tomorrow.

"Melanie was supposed to come to the precinct in Hamshire today, but I got a call from my contact there that she didn't show. He wondered if maybe Melanie got mixed up and landed herself in Sweetwater Falls, thinking she needed to talk only to me, like Jeremy does."

I fan out the tablecloth, smoothing out the bumps in the fabric so the vendor tomorrow has a blank canvas on which to display their wares. "It sounds like Melanie doesn't want to talk to the police," I offer. "Can't blame her. I mean, has there been a funeral for her father? It's a little insensitive for anyone to ask her to drive out of town to be questioned for her father's murder when it's all this fresh."

Logan shrugs. "The longer we wait, the colder the trail to the killer gets." He raises his hands in surrender. "I agree, it's a crummy situation. But no one brings in a suspect assuming the worst, especially if there's personal loss involved. We're not monsters. We just need to cross her off the list of suspects, which isn't all that long."

My mouth pulls to the side as I tug one end of the tablecloth to make sure it hangs evenly. "Then why didn't Melanie go to the Hamshire precinct?"

The question lingers in the air with no answer in sight. The only person who can tell us that is Melanie herself, who doesn't seem to want to come anywhere near our small town.

The door opens, letting a blast of icy air into the drafty gymnasium. Everyone instinctively backs away, but then rushes forward when the Live Forever Club enters holding bags that are overflowing with yarn.

I love that a dozen people rush to help the three women I admire most with their bags, offering their elbows for the women to lean on if they need the support.

Marianne comes in after them, stomping the snow off

her boots. Her arms are full, so I rush to help her. "Yikes. It looks like it's really coming down out there." I dust a few flakes from her coat.

Marianne shivers. "So cold. We're in the thick of it now. I told them that we shouldn't go out in the snowstorm, but you know how they are. Once they get an idea in their heads, there's no stopping them. I figured I would drive them, but I regret it." Marianne raises her voice to address everyone. "You should all seriously consider heading home now. A snowstorm is starting up, and the weather forecast says it won't be letting up any time soon." Her scarf has white plastered across most of the red yarn, making her look like a precious snowwoman. Her nose is pink, and her teeth are chattering.

Rip's face falls. "No. The storm wasn't supposed to roll in until Sunday."

Marianne casts him a wry look through her shivering. "You're welcome to go outside and reason with Mother Nature. I'm betting she'll tell you the same thing I am now."

Karen sets her bags down on the nearest table and rubs her hands together. "Three more trips should do it." Then she sighs dramatically. "If only some strapping young men could help a poor old woman unload her car."

Logan trots to the exit alongside Dwight, who has been here since noon.

Karen winks at me, smiling at the help that comes if only you ask for it. "How are you, honey cake?"

"I'm alright. I didn't know the book club was doing an event this big. I mean, I've seen the projects you ladies have been working on, but this is... There are twenty-four booths set up. I didn't realize there would be so much for sale tomorrow."

Agnes moves one of her bags to the floor behind her table. "It's our book club's only fundraiser. It sets our budget for the entire year, so we like to make it a big event. The more we rake in tomorrow, the bigger the budget."

I nod and help her unpack her bags. There are blankets of every color, solids and rainbow and color schemes to match every single living room décor one can imagine. Each one is folded with care and placed on the table, giving each blanket its best opportunity to go to a new home.

I gape at the collection. "Agnes, how many blankets are there? These are huge and gorgeous! Wow! I had no idea you made this many." The blankets keep on coming. They have different stitching patterns that look flawless. There is a mixture of love and expertise radiating from each piece, making every new thing I pull out of the bag my new favorite item.

I am careful not to let anything hit the ground, folding each piece so the patterns can stand out and catch the buyers' eyes.

Winifred's movements are stiff as she motions for Dennis and Laura to move one of the tables over to sit beside Agnes' display. "There's not enough space at this one. We need a double. My hats are smaller, so Agnes can use part of my table."

Rip throws his hands up, exasperated when anyone messes with his perfect plans for an event. "Now it's uneven! Winnie, I know the Live Forever Club wanted three tables, and I gave them to you, but if you push them together, what's that going to do to the balance of the room? It'll look like a flea market! We're going for a quality showing, here."

Winnie pinches Rip's round cheek and then pats it twice, smiling when he winces at the chill in her fingers. "We'll make it look nice, Rip. Don't you worry."

Rip harrumphs at her, no doubt flustered that the Live Forever Club does what they like, and they usually get away with it, being that they give so much cheer to the town.

Winnie directs Dennis again, then starts taking out her collection of hats and fanning them out on the end of the table.

"I can help with that," I tell her. "You girls sit down and get yourselves warm. I'll set this up."

They don't need to be told twice. All three women pull up chairs while I take directions, sorting their items in categories and then putting them in color order, which apparently is very specific.

After Logan and Dwight drop off the rest of the bags (I hope that's all there is. We might need another table),

Dwight makes his way to Rip and starts speaking in hushed tones.

Logan shakes the snow off his jacket a few feet away from the crafts he just hauled in, which I can tell the ladies appreciate. They pepper Logan with questions about how he's doing and is he eating enough until Rip's voice carries above the din.

"Alright, people. Listen up. I hate to do this because we are nowhere near finished, but apparently the snowstorm didn't get the memo that we have a fair to put on. The roads are getting slippery, so we have to call it a night. Thank you for your help, and I hope to see you all here two hours before the fair starts at noon tomorrow, so we can put the finishing touches on this event."

I groan internally. This was supposed to be a two-hour commitment total, but the workload has been multiplying at a rapid pace.

I grab up my purse and slide my arms into my coat. "I can take Winnie home, Marianne. Do you want me to drop off Karen on the way?"

Marianne nods. "Could you? That would be great. I don't want to be out in this mess a minute longer than I have to be. I'll take Agnes home."

Logan raises his hand. "I've got a truck. I can take Karen home. Then Charlotte, you can head straight home with Winnie. There's no telling how your car will handle the roads. And it's no trouble for me to take Agnes, too. She's on my way. Marianne, I can't imagine you'll want to be out a second longer than you have to be."

Marianne surprises an "oof" sound from Logan when she throws her arms around his neck. "Thank you! I'm not built for the cold. I owe you a hot apple cider tomorrow at the fair."

Logan chuckles. "I'm going to hold you to that." He proffers his elbow to Karen, even though we are nowhere near finished setting up their booth. "Shall we?"

Karen raises her bony chin like the queen she is. "That would be delightful. Thank you, dear." She kisses my cheek in parting, and Logan does the same.

Not quite the date I had in mind for tonight, but it's just as well. I would rather we were all safe at home than fighting with the weather.

Instead of rushing out the door, Marianne walks beside me as I move toward the exit, with Agnes and Winnie tagging behind. Marianne keeps her voice low. "Jeremy called me," she admits, an uncomfortable look on her face. Even beneath her scarf and rosy cheeks, I can tell she does not want this to have happened. "He wants the ring back. My engagement ring."

My eyes widen as my steps slow to a halt. "What? He actually asked for it back? He cheated! The marriage didn't happen because of him!"

Marianne shakes her head. "I don't want it. I don't want it in my house. I don't want any money I could get from selling it. He can have it back." Her lips firm. "I wish I had never taken it in the first place." Before I can offer up any semblance of sympathy or pep talk, she reaches into her pocket and pulls out a small jewelry box. She takes my hand and rests it in my palm. "He's still staying at The Snuggle Inn, which is on your way home. Can I ask you the biggest favor?"

My eyes widen, but I keep my mouth shut. I don't want to see Jeremy, and I really don't want anything to do with a diamond ring that might easily fall out of my pocket.

Marianne blinks at me with her big brown eyes. "Could you stop by The Snuggle Inn on your way home and drop it off to him? I want to give it back, but I don't want to have to see him."

I gape at her, but before I can muster up any sort of argument, the best friend side of me is nodding and putting the small box in my jacket pocket. "Of course. Anything you need. In ten minutes, it will be taken care of."

Marianne exhales, and I realize then how hard this must be for her. "Thank you."

Without permitting another second to pass, I wrap my arms around her slight frame and hold her tight. I want to tell her that she is brave and better off—both of which are true. I want to tell her that I am proud of her for moving on from a past that was far grimmer than her bright future promises to be. I want to tell her she is amazing, but all those sentiments wrap themselves into one simple sentence. "I love you so much."

Marianne sniffles in my arms, her chin resting on my shoulder. "This is hard," she admits. "This whole thing has been hard."

I nod, holding her closer so I can hopefully bear a small portion of her pain. I don't want her to have to carry the full weight of it alone.

I walk her to her car, determined to get this next task done so Sweetwater Falls can be rid of Jeremy once and for all.

17

RECEPTIONIST DOWN

The drive to The Snuggle Inn shouldn't take more than ten minutes, but in this snowstorm, I am grateful when we reach our destination twenty minutes later.

I cut the engine and turn to my aunt. "I know the wise thing to do is go straight home, but I can't let this diamond engagement ring sit in my pocket all night long. I'll misplace it, or something bad will happen. I need to get this done for Marianne, then we're going straight home."

Aunt Winnie bats her mitten-clad hand at my fretting. "Don't you worry, honey cake. I agree with you. When Marianne needs help, we're all for it. A few minutes' delay isn't going to hurt a thing."

I sincerely hope she's right, because the snow is coming in thick sheets. Even walking to through the parking lot into the entrance of The Snuggle Inn is more of an effort that I would like it to be. I expect Aunt Winnie to stay in the car and wait for me, but she comes in beside me, clinging to my arm to ensure she doesn't lose her footing.

No one is at the front desk, so we meander into the dining room, which is also empty. It's eight o'clock at night, so it's no surprise that everything is closed down. The guests are no doubt turning in for the night inside their warm rooms, enjoying the view of the snow from safely inside the bed and breakfast.

My mouth pulls to the side. "Well, I can't exactly leave the ring on the counter here with a note. Should I go upstairs and start knocking on doors?"

Aunt Winnie takes matters into her own hands, which is no great surprise. She shuffles behind the reception desk and flips open the appointment book. "Ah. Jeremy is in room nine."

I tsk her as if I am unimpressed with her constant ability to write her own rules instead of following the social norms laid out for everyone. "You're not supposed to be behind there!"

Winnie chortles. "Oh, my. For a second, I thought you were serious. This is nothing. It didn't even involve breaking and entering." She flips the page of the appointment book. Then she picks up a pen and starts writing in the little boxes. "The Live Forever Club is getting a free room next Wednesday. Feel like joining us? We deserve a little break after all that knitting."

I balk at her gall. "You can't do that!"

Winnie points to the book. "I think I just did. The manager signed off on it and everything." She motions to the decent copy of Lenny's signature, which is on another box where a room received a discount.

I chuckle at her wicked antics. "You are positively out of control, Aunt Winnie."

My great-aunt straightens, her chin proudly raised. "I certainly hope I am never controlled. I can't imagine a more sinfully boring life."

I shake my head at her as I move up the steps, leaving Winifred to her mischief.

My steps are quiet as I pad down the upstairs hallway, where the rooms are.

I'm not sure I've been up to the actual rooms, or if I have, I didn't take note of the details before. There are a few pictures on the walls of nature scenes that look local to the town. In fact, I think I have been to that particular spot where the sun sets over the fishing pond.

The hallway is lit by two sconces that shed a cozy illumination, so I don't lose my way. When I come to Room 9, I knock lightly on the door. "Jeremy?" I stage whisper, hoping my voice doesn't carry. I don't want to wake anyone or impede on their quiet evening.

I hear a woman's voice shrieking inside in response, so I knock a little louder. "Jeremy, I have something of yours."

There is a banging sound behind the door that makes me jump, followed by a man's pained "oof!" and then nothing else.

I knock again, now worried because that loud thump didn't sound like a stubbed toe. "Jeremy?"

My heartrate picks up, not because I care about Jeremy or feel protective of him in any way, but because I am certain there is something nefarious happening on the other side of this door.

I try the handle, but of course it is locked.

I flit to the staircase and race down, landing myself in the lobby once more. I sprint behind the desk, foregoing the rules I know should keep me on the guest's side of the desk, and not where only employees are allowed.

Aunt Winnie shuts the appointment book and takes in my pinched eyebrows. "Everything okay, honey cake?"

"I need a key to Jeremy's room. He's not in there alone. I heard a loud thump that didn't sound like nothing."

Aunt Winifred turns behind her to the wall of keys, but then frowns. "Huh. There's usually a spare to each room here if it's only a single in the room. Why would Jeremy need two keys? The other one for Room 9 isn't on the hook, where it should be."

I don't have all the pieces put together as to why this should worry me, but it spikes my fear all the same. An urgency rises in me that pinches my voice. "Winnie, why is there no one at this desk? We have to get into Room 9. I am positive something bad is happening. Who is supposed to be working the desk?"

Winifred opens a second notebook and flips to today's date. "Here we go. Looks like Lydia was on the schedule for tonight. Maybe check the office over there?" she suggests, motioning to the hallway on the other side of the lobby, where guests don't have reason to visit.

I've been in Lenny's office before, so I know the way. I move quickly out of the lobby and turn the corner, but before I can make it more than two steps toward my destination, a gasp flings from my lips. "Oh! Winnie, call for help!" I race to the body on the floor. Though I don't know this woman personally, I have seen her before, working the front desk on occasion. "Winnie, hurry!"

I can hear Aunt Winifred talking into the phone, so I know help will be on the way. I lightly slap Lydia's cheek, checking for any blood or obvious marks.

On her forehead looks to be the beginnings of a goose egg that might prove problematic. I'm guessing that's the source of her laying on the ground, unconscious.

My fingers fish for her pulse. Gratitude rushes out of me in a gust when I feel a steady beat stir beneath my touch. "Oh, thank goodness!" Though Lydia isn't awake, she is alive.

I brush her black bangs from her forehead, careful not to touch what looks like a very sore spot. "Lydia? Wake up, hun."

Aunt Winifred comes to stand beside where I am kneeling. She fishes in her purse and pulls something small out. She unwraps it and hands it to me. "Stick this under her nose. See if that wakes her. The paramedics are on their way, along with the police, but the dispatcher mentioned there might be a delay because of the storm.

I study the thing in my hand with confusion. "A cough drop? What's that going to do?"

"Trust me. Those things are stronger than smelling salts. Unwrap it and stick it under her nose. See if that brings some light to her eyes."

I do as I am instructed, my fingers clumsy with panic. I drop the lozenge twice before I manage to get the paper off and shove it under Lydia's nose. "Here! Oh, please wake up!"

The thing smells terrible. There's a strong menthol to it, but there's also a bad medicine quality that makes me scrunch my nose. "Oh, that smells terrible!"

Winnie nods. "Tastes bad, too, but it helps a sore throat in a pinch."

It takes a few beats, but sure enough, the cough drop does the trick.

Lydia's lashes flutter as she blinks the room into focus. "Huh? Why am I... Why are you..." She touches her forehead and then winces.

"Easy," I warn Lydia as she tries to sit up. I offer my help, and finally, she is able to sag against the wall. Her business casual clothes are wrinkled but unbloodied. Her hands press to the floor on either side of her to keep her curvy body from tipping. "Cupcake girl?" she addresses me with confusion. "What are you doing here?"

I like that label. "Charlotte," I offer. "I came to see one

of your guests, but I found you on the floor. Tell us what happened. Who did this to you?"

Lydia shakes her head, but then cringes, immediately touching her temple, no doubt to stop the room from spinning. "I don't know. I mean, I saw her, but I don't know who she is. A woman. City girl, by the looks of her shoes. She wanted to see one of our guests, but he wouldn't come down. She asked me to let her into his room, but of course, we don't do that."

Lydia swoons. Her eyes roll back, so I lower her back to the floor, making sure she is lying supine.

I hold her hand as I kneel at her side. Even though I don't know this woman more than being able to state her name and occupation, I hold her gaze with a promise that everything will be okay. "I'm right here. An ambulance is on its way."

The woman's eyes water. "I didn't see it coming. She grabbed me by my hair and slammed my head onto the desk. That's the last thing I remember." Lydia glances around, as if just realizing she is in the hallway. "She must have dragged me over here."

Aunt Winnie's hand on my shoulder is cold and grips firmly. "Is there a master key? I think whoever it is took the spare one to Jeremy's room. He might be in danger."

Lydia fumbles around on her hip, dipping her hand into her pocket and pulling out a key ring. "On here. Call the police."

"Already done," Winifred assures her. "They're on their way."

I take the keys from Lydia and stand. "Stay with her, Aunt Winnie. I'm going to get Jeremy out of here."

Hesitation crosses my great-aunt's features. Normally I am the one preaching caution while she is racing headfirst into danger. But this time, she stills my actions with her hand on my wrist. "We should wait for the police."

I shake my head. "I can't do that. I know what I heard. Someone is in there with Jeremy. If it's the person who killed Ray, then I might already be too late." I motion to Lydia. "Stay with her."

Aunt Winifred doesn't nod but she also doesn't continue her quest to introduce me to reason.

I take that as my opportunity to bolt, so I do exactly that.

I race down the hallway, through the lobby and up the steps, rushing past the two spots of light on the walls, not stopping until I reach Room 9.

I know I am about to find the famous country star in some sort of disrepair.

My clumsy fingers are charged with anxiety, so I go through four keys and drop the whole set twice before the correct one shoves itself into the lock, springing the door open.

The lamplit room is in disarray. There is a chair knocked over and clothes strewn about the place. I gasp when I take a step further inside and see none other than

Jeremy Johnson sprawled out on the floor, blood flowing from his mouth and nose.

I rush toward his side, fearing the worst, but before I get more than three steps inside, a woman leaps out from the bathroom and knocks me across the shoulder with a heavy clothing iron.

I let out a bleat of alarm as I stumble and slam into the wall.

Though I do not recognize the woman who assaulted me, that hardly seems to matter to her.

Vengeance gleams in her gaze as she raises the iron once more, determined to keep me from helping Jeremy, if it's not already too late for such things.

I should have gone straight home instead of stopping here. I should have at least stayed downstairs with Aunt Winifred and waited for the police to arrive.

But none of those options matter now as the woman takes another swing at me, bashing my arm once more.

18

RAY MONTAGNE'S KILLER

Going straight home after we were dismissed from setting up for the knitting fair at the high school gymnasium would have been the smart thing to do. Winter storms are one headache but being bashed across the shoulder with a clothing iron is quite the ordeal.

I blink focus into the lamplit room, wondering why I chose to come in here when I thought Jeremy might be in danger. I owe him nothing, yet here I am, bursting into his room when he needs help.

I don't want to be the one helping him, yet here I go.

The woman who slammed me on the shoulder with the iron is a total stranger to me. She has dyed hot pink hair to match her lipstick and penciled-in eyebrows. She looks to be about my age, though dressed like an out of towner in tight bedazzled jeans, heels, and a V-neck sweater that looks about three sizes too small for her busty frame.

"Are you sleeping with him, too?" she shouts at me.

"What?" Nothing could disgust me more. "No! I came to give him something."

My response only seems to fuel the woman's displeasure. She takes another swing at me with the iron, missing my face when I duck. The iron carves a skidded hole into the drywall behind me, lodging the thing there so she has to tug at it.

I am not skilled at fighting, but I know I have to learn quick if I am going to get out of here with my head attached to my neck.

Before she can yank the iron from the wall, I bend in half and slam into her midsection. My force knocks her off her balance and pins her to the opposite after she stumbles backward. "Ouch!" she exclaims, as if she can't believe I would fight back.

My shoulder smarts from where she struck me on her first swing when I entered the room, but I can't focus on that now. I need to get Jeremy out of here, or I have the feeling he will go out in much the same way his manager left this world.

"Leave him alone!" I growl as I try to keep her pinned in place. My frame is smashed against hers so she can't jerk her body off the wall. "Why would you think you could get away with beating him up like this? What did he do to you?"

She is strong, her hands erratic as they scrabble against my arms and my face. She scratches with a vehemence that makes me wish I hadn't come up here in the first place.

"You should know! You're his ex-fiancée, aren't you. You're Marianne! You came here to get him back!"

"What? Gross! Ah!" I cry out as the woman shoves me backward, giving her a second to catch her bearings while I lose my own. "I'm not..."

The woman grabs me by the hair and stomps toward Jeremy's unconscious body. "*I'm* his girlfriend! Doesn't anybody understand that?"

I put the pieces together, though I'm not sure that matters now. If I die before the police get here and she escapes, her identity won't be made known to those who can actually do something about it.

I claw the wall to steady myself as best I can while she drags me toward Jeremy.

"What is so hard about keeping your hands off other people's men? I mean, you understand. He cheated on you. But that was a *you* problem. We have a connection, Jeremy and me. We have the music. We don't need you coming in and wrecking everything. I have enough to deal with on the tour."

I grope at her grip on my hair, trying get her hand off me. "You're crazy! I'm not..."

"I know Jeremy's patterns. And I know you're not the only one he's cheating on me with. He's seeing Julia, you realize. So if you thought you were special, you're wrong. I'm dealing with the both of you now, and then I'll deal with her."

I finally yank myself free of her clutches, stumbling away and accidentally tripping over Jeremy's arm. I fall on the floor, my elbow smarting as it skids across the hard surface.

"I'm not Marianne! And she wants nothing to do with him. Melanie, you can't honestly believe..."

Melanie Montagne scoffs, huffing her indignation. "You think I don't know he cheats? Well, I do."

Tears spring to her eyes as she grabs up the desk lamp in her fist, tearing the cord out of the wall so we are bathed in shadow. I see only what the glow of the moon and the snow outside want me to see.

It is the wrong time for Jeremy to stir, but his groan floats to my ears as he turns his head from left to right.

Melanie's voice catches as she steps toward me. "We were happy. I had it under control. He was going to be on the tour with me, so booked that we would spend every day together for the next two years. All he had to do was sign the contract."

I need to keep her talking. I have to buy more time for the police to get here. I'm not sure Jeremy can survive another attack from her, beaten up as he looks. Even in the shadows, I can make out the puffiness of his busted lip and his eye that is swollen completely shut.

"There was a contract?" I ask, though I already know as much.

"Yes! Do you know how long I had to work on Daddy before he caved? It took so much effort to convince him to sign Jeremy for such a packed tour, but *I* made it happen." She lets a handful of sobs loose. "I fought for our relationship. Then he doesn't want to sign the contract? I'm not enough of a lure to put a pen in his hand so he can sign on the dotted line? That's all I get? A 'let me take a night to think about it,' which was really a 'let me take a night to hook up with the woman I've been seeing behind your back.'"

She announces the scandal, and I know I am supposed to gasp as if this is the first time I am aware of what a scumbag Jeremy is. "That's horrible," I offer, and I truly mean it. "He was cheating on you?"

She looms over us. I know if I make any sudden moves, it will spark her to knock me over the head with the lamp in her hand, so I stay down near Jeremy, and keep her talking as best I can. "I can't believe he cheated!"

I sure can, but I don't say that.

Melanie's emotion fuses her words together. "We are meant to be! I don't care if he can't see it yet. We belong together."

My head swims but I fight to stay in the moment. "How did your father die, then? You got Jeremy the contract you wanted, but then what?"

Melanie's mouth twists with disdain. "He gave Jeremy

the offer, but Jeremy wouldn't sign it! I knew. I knew it when Julia told me she was going to spend the night in Jacksonville, which was where Jeremy told me he would be for the night. He was cheating with Julia! She's not even a singer!"

As if that matters.

"That must have been so hurtful." And that part, I truly mean. "He shouldn't have cheated."

"No, he shouldn't have. So I went to my dad and asked him to kick Julia off the tour. We don't need a makeup artist. Jeremy and I need the time together now, with no distractions. I needed Jeremy away from Julia. I told my daddy to fire Julia and kick her off the tour, but he refused!" Melanie's voice is shrill, and somehow, I can perfectly picture her demanding a pony from her father in the same childish manner. "I warned him that I was unhappy. I told him this was what I needed him to do, and he said no!"

She announces her father's verdict as if it is some great scandal she cannot believe.

"What happened then?" My voice turns grave. "Melanie, what did you do?"

"I didn't mean to! I was angry because Daddy made me that way! It's not like he couldn't make my problems with Jeremy and Julia go away. He refused to be helpful, so I got angry. I didn't mean to get so mad, but before I knew it, my hands were around his throat. The contract was no good to me if Julia would be on the tour with us. Jeremy might have already left me for her! So I shoved it down his throat. Daddy choked and... so I... And then..." She hiccups as rage turns into grief. I am not sure she is capable of having a full-blown conscience, but there is a ping of regret I hear in her sobs. It's as if this is the first time she is admitting to herself all she has done in the misguided name of love.

The lamp drops to the floor as she covers her mouth with her hand. Her tears flow freely now.

I don't have time to feel bad for her plight. I know I have to take my opportunity while her guard is down. I glance around the room in search of anything that might be useful to arm myself with in anticipation of an escape.

Everything is soft and unmenacing. There are pillows, clothing and a bedspread. Nothing that can do actual damage, except the lamp, which is too close to her for me to grab. I can't run out, because not only is she standing in the way of my exit, but that would mean I would have to leave Jeremy behind, since he is in no shape for a speedy escape.

Jeremy groans again, though I wish he was still passed out. His sound draws Melanie's attention from her own grief to his supine form sprawled out on the floor at her feet.

She sucks in a quick breath. "Jeremy wasn't happy to see me." She shakes her head in a rapid motion. "Why wasn't he happy to see me? Is there someone else?"

"Other than Julia? I can't imagine there is. Marianne doesn't want anything to do with him."

Melanie motions around. "Then why did he insist on coming to this Podunk town in the middle of nowhere? Why drive my father's body across state lines here, if not to reunite with his ex-fiancée?"

I almost feel sorry for this woman whose priorities and self-worth as so severely turned around.

I feel for her, but that compassion is mired by my need to escape the crazy that has so thoroughly taken her over.

"You murdered your father," I say aloud, though I should probably not confront her with that hard fact or obvious condemnation when she is so thoroughly vexed.

Melanie's lower lip firms. "You don't understand. You've never been in love."

I don't argue because I don't know if what I feel for Logan can be classified as something so grand as love. "I don't know about that, but I do know that love shouldn't drive you to murder. You loved your father, didn't you? Yet you killed him."

Melanie's breath quakes. "He didn't understand," she repeats, as if that is a good enough reason for any of this to have happened.

Jeremy groans, but this time, his one good eye opens. "What... I..."

Melanie's nostrils flare. It is then that I know I have to act. I cannot wait for the authorities to arrive. I have to do something now. She is no longer a sad, jilted woman; Melanie is a killer with no regrets.

It's now or most assuredly never.

Though my gait is unsteady, I lunge for the woman who brought so much drama into my precious small town. I am determined that this will be the last night Melanie Montagne will ever set foot in Sweetwater Falls.

Melanie screams when I jump up and leap over Jeremy, squandering no time at all as I tackle her around the waist. I knock her backwards, slamming her to the floor.

She struggles against me, but I am determined to end this madness tonight. I reach for the lamp she was going to use to clobber me. I lift it overhead, my knees on either side of her hips as I steady myself to keep her in place.

"Stop! You don't understand! Jeremy and I belong together!"

I cannot stomach another word. Though I don't want it to have to come to this, I slam the base of the lamp down, cracking it over her head.

Finally, Melanie's spoiled excuses come to a stop. Her chin lolls to the side and her body goes limp beneath mine.

19

THE MISTAKES WE MAKE

*I*f I have ever been more grateful to see Logan in all my life, I cannot recall it. When he barrels into the room half a minute after I knocked Melanie unconscious with the lamp, I nearly sob my relief when he comes into view.

Logan turns on the light, gasping at the scene as another officer races into the room on his heels. "Charlotte, are you okay?"

My lower lip quivers as I try to think through how to answer something like that.

No, I'm not okay. I will never be okay so long as people like this are allowed to roam free and do as they please with other people's lives.

No, I am not okay that I risked my life to save a man who was so terrible to Marianne.

No, I am not okay that I had to hear the sordid details of a relationship gone horribly wrong.

But I don't say any of that. "I'm okay," I offer weakly. "Melanie did it," I tell him in a croaky voice. "She killed her father."

Logan crouches on the other side of Melanie's head so he can get in my eyeline. "And I take it this is Melanie Montagne, Jeremy's girlfriend?"

I nod. "He cheated. She knew it. She wanted him all to herself. Her dad couldn't make that happen, so she killed her father." I motion behind me. "She... And I came in and saw him on the floor. Logan, it was..."

Logan's head tilts to the side. "I think you've done a fair amount of sleuthing for· today. How about I get you out of this room, and you let me do the easy part of handcuffing and arresting and whatnot."

My lower lip quivers. I nod at what sounds like the best offer in the universe. "Yes. Yes, please."

I cling to Logan as he helps me off Melanie, bringing me into the hallway while the other officer cuffs the woman on the floor.

The second officer nods toward Jeremy, who is still lying down. "The ambulance is on the way."

"Lydia!" I shout. "Lydia was knocked out downstairs. Aunt Winnie is with her. She needs medical attention, too."

Logan nods, his arm curving around my waist as he steadies me with his other hand. "I caught the abbreviated version on my way up the stairs to get to you. Ambulance is on the way."

Once we get into the hallway, I sink into his arms. "It was horrible! I don't want to risk my life to save Jeremy! He's the worst!"

"I know," Logan coos, his voice gentle. His cadence is a beautiful balm on my soul after being subjected to the shrieking of a spoiled woman mere minutes ago. "It's all over now. We will take her in, and she will pay for what she did to her father, and for what she did to you and Jeremy."

I nod, then bury my face in Logan's shoulder. "I can't imagine being in a relationship like that. I won't ever cheat on you, okay? If I want out, I'll say it."

Logan nods. "Agreed. But I don't want out. In fact, I'm fairly certain I will never want out." He holds the back of my head, his cheek cold on my temple.

I am so grateful for the path that led us to each other. However long it took me to realize such a stunning man could possibly look my way, it was worth the wait if it landed us here. His tender embrace engulfs me, granting me a sliver of peace to hold onto in the midst of the chaos that lies a few feet away.

Aunt Winifred's voice carries down the hall. "Logan, bring Charlotte here."

Logan's steps are slow as he walks me toward my aunt. He sits me down in a chair behind reception and gets in my eyeline, taking in whatever damage Melanie did in the fight. He thumbs at my arm. "You're hurt."

"Melanie knocked me in the shoulder with an iron." I glance at my arm. "My cardigan is ripped! Doggone. Agnes made this for me."

Aunt Winifred hisses. "I knew I should have made you stay away from that room! There's brave and then there's flat out endangering yourself. Don't you know my heart can't take it if anything happened to you?" Her sea green eyes glisten with unshed tears.

I rarely see this fragile side of her. Aunt Winnie always seems in control of every reaction. She's usually ready for anything.

I guess she's not ready to lose me.

I feel the same way.

"Go on, Logan. Go be a cop. I'll stay with my girl." She holds onto my hand while she calls over her shoulder. "Karen, do me a favor? Can you get some ice from the kitchen for Lydia's head? And another bag of ice for Charlotte's shoulder."

I am surprised to see Karen pop into the lobby from around the corner. "Of course, dear. I can't believe this night. You two are out of my sight for less than half an hour, and everything falls apart." Karen mumbles unhappily to herself as she crosses through the lobby and into the dining room, which is the quickest route into the kitchen.

"How is Karen here?" I ask, still holding to my aunt's silky hand.

"Logan was driving her home when he got the call about the attack. He didn't want to waste time dropping Agnes and Karen off, so he brought them along. Karen said that makes them honorary police officers." Winifred shakes her head with an attempt at a smile. "I'm not sure we should burst her bubble with the truth just yet." She kisses my forehead. "Agnes is with Lydia."

I cradle my head in my free hand, holding myself back from either crying or ranting, I'm not sure which.

Winifred moves my head to her midsection, holding me to her so I don't drift.

I sigh, beyond tired of this whole thing. "I can't believe something so terrible happened here. Why couldn't they keep their crazy relationship out of Sweetwater Falls?"

Aunt Winifred runs her fingernails through my blonde curls. "Some people need to control situations that aren't meant for them to have a say in. They learn eventually, but it's not always a smooth road to the reckoning."

Guilt weights my shoulders. "I did that. I tried to control the situation when I thought Marianne was dating Jeremy again. I did all I could to keep them apart instead of letting her be an adult capable of making her own decisions." I groan at my many missteps. "And Marianne was perfect all along. I made myself crazy over nothing, just like Melanie."

Aunt Winifred kisses the top of my head. "The good

news is that you're learning from a small mistake. Melanie is going to jail tonight, and something tells me she's not going to learn that she did the wrong thing for quite some time." She smooths back my curls again. "Learn the lessons and be grateful for the ride that brought you there."

I let her wisdom ping in my heart. I cannot imagine a life better than one with my Aunt Winnie and the quirky people of Sweetwater Falls.

Aunt Winifred holds my hand as Karen comes out with a bundle of ice twisted in a rag. Karen presses the cold compress to my shoulder as paramedics rush into The Snuggle Inn, prepared to clean up the mess that swept unbidden into our precious small town.

20

NO REGRETS

The entire town was crushed that the Knit Your Heart Out fair had to be postponed a whole week. But with the snowstorm and the horrid events at The Snuggle Inn, no one argued that the fair be put off until the town could properly celebrate.

Plus, that gave Agnes, Winifred and Karen more time to make extra knitted projects, which apparently, these women can crank out without breaking a sweat.

"Those are pretty," Marianne sighs as she leans in to smell the roses on the kitchen counter again. She sniffs the petals every time she passes the tall vase as if it's the first time she has ever smelled a flower. "I can't believe the tour company sent you flowers for getting to the bottom of Ray Montagne's murder and saving Jeremy's life. They look beautiful in Winifred's kitchen, too."

The tour company sent me flowers and an autographed copy of one of Jeremy's albums.

I kept the flowers and threw the album in the trash.

The white petals are beautiful, especially surrounded by baby's breath. They sit in front of my goldfish's bowl, so Buttercream has a nice change of scenery. My cute fish flicks her tail as she swims, looking at Marianne as if excited her friend as come home to play.

In fact, Marianne has come here to check on me, not Buttercream, as she's done every day since the incident.

Marianne keeps her head turned from me but lowers her chin as she speaks. Before her mouth opens, I know what she is going to say. "It's all my fault. You had a huge mark on your shoulder from the fight that I sent you into. You wouldn't have gone there at all and none of this would have happened if I hadn't asked you to take the ring back to Jeremy."

I turn in my chair at the kitchen table, admiring the cheery yellow of the cupboards even though Marianne's disposition is quite the opposite. "But if you hadn't asked me to take the ring to Jeremy, I wouldn't have caught Melanie in the act. She might have killed Jeremy and gotten away with killing her own father. Because you asked for help, Jeremy is alive, and Melanie is in jail. I think that's the best outcome anyone has ever had after asking someone to run an errand for them."

Marianne turns her chin to shoot me a wry look. "You know it was more than a simple errand I asked you to run for me. And in the middle of a snowstorm, no less! I feel awful."

"Well, I feel fine. Honestly. My shoulder doesn't hurt anymore, and I'm grateful the truth came out. Granted, I wish Jeremy had kept his drama out of Sweetwater Falls, but that's out of my control."

Aunt Winifred comes down the steps in an outfit that knocks the air from my lungs. "Okay, ladies. I am ready to be admired."

My mouth drops open and Marianne claps for the showstopper that is my aunt's dress.

The entire thing is crocheted out of light green yarn that matches the color of her pretty eyes. The capped sleeves have lace trim around the edges, making her look like a princess. The bodice is fitted with a collar that goes up her neck with pearl buttons along the side. The skirt flows to an inch above her shoes with a scalloped hem along the bottom. The waist has a belt around it that is a ribbon, reading, "Read. Knit. Repeat."

Marianne applauds the spectacle. "Gorgeous! I forgot about the details on the neck. So pretty!"

Aunt Winnie indulges us in a twirl. "I wear this dress exactly once a year, but every time I feel like it's the first time."

I gape at the details and the perfect fit. "Did you make that?"

Aunt Winifred nods. "Of course I did. If you want to

sell something, you have to look like you know what you're doing. This dress says exactly that."

I stand, grabbing up her knitting bag and her purse. "I can't wait to see all the items. You three were very hush-hush about the box we delivered yesterday to the gymnasium. I still can't believe you made me wait outside so I couldn't see what it was."

"I told you what it was," Winifred scolds me, her chin lifted. "It's a surprise."

I snicker as I lean over and smell the roses once more before I make my way to the front door. "I can't wait to take it all in. I love town events."

Marianne helps Aunt Winnie with her coat and then slides on her own while I grab for mine. "I'm just glad Jeremy is gone. It was worth it to push back the fair a week to make sure we could enjoy it without him." Marianne leans against the wall beside the door as she toes on her winter boots. "I remember the last time we went to the Knit Your Heart Out fair together when we were engaged. We got there late because he was working on a song and didn't want to be interrupted. Then when we got there, he ditched me in the first five minutes to go hang with some of his old high school friends."

My upper lip curls. "And you dated him why? He's the worst." I cringe at my words. "I probably shouldn't say that about him, being that he's still all banged up and whatnot."

Marianne's voice is quiet. "He's okay though? I don't

want him near me, but I don't wish bodily harm on him either."

"That makes one of us," I grumble.

Aunt Winifred chuckles at my sass. "I think all three of us are in the right place at the right time. The mistakes we've made, the plans that fell through, the moments we wish we could undo—they've all led us here. We're together, which is the best place I can think to be." Aunt Winifred kisses my cheek, and then Marianne's. "Regrets are meant to be studied and then buried. We learn from them, and we move on with firmer footing."

Marianne nods, and I can see her committing this wisdom to memory. "I like that."

"I like *you*," I tell my best friend. "And I like Carlos, so keep him around for as long as he is good to you."

A genuine smile spreads across Marianne's face. "I plan on it. He's meeting us there, on time, and not with his high school buddies."

I smile as I open the front door for us, ready to enjoy the better parts of Sweetwater Falls. I want to appreciate every moment it gives me and dive headfirst into a future without regrets.

With Marianne and the Live Forever Club by my side, I'm guessing that is exactly the kind of future I am destined to enjoy.

21

KNIT YOUR HEART OUT

The gymnasium is packed fifteen minutes into the event, and the crowd doesn't thin out even an hour into the afternoon. I have never seen so many knitted things in one place before, but it seems that everyone has dressed for the occasion. Items bought from previous Knit Your Heart Out fairs stand out on every single person in the gymnasium. Even Logan sports a scarf that he refuses to take off, even though it is quite warm inside, what with all the people milling about.

Carlos has been glued to Marianne's side all afternoon. When Marianne jumps and exclaims, "The special items are about to be unveiled at the auction!" Carlos nearly drops his cup of hot apple cider.

"Do we get numbered paddles? How does the auction work?" I ask as Logan and I move toward the far side of the gymnasium where a foot-tall stage has been set up. There are various tables on the stage behind the podium where Rip has set himself up with his best auctioneer outfit—a red and white knitted suitcoat paired with beige trousers.

I guess that's what an auctioneer looks like in Rip's imagination.

Works for me.

I have been wanting to see what is under those black coverings on the stage since I came into the fair, and finally, it's time. "I'm going to be disappointed if a carnival complete with clowns doesn't leap out from under those cloths," I tell Marianne. "The suspense is killing me."

"I know! I can't believe the Live Forever Club wouldn't tell us what the secret project is."

Carlos glances around. "Charlotte's right. There aren't any paddles. Shouldn't there be paddles at an auction?"

Marianne shrugs. "Everyone knows everyone. We don't need numbers. We just shout out our bid."

I chew on my lower lip. The anticipation is killing me. "The Live Forever Club's booth is nearly sold out, by the way." I squeeze Marianne's hand. "Did you see that?"

Marianne nods. "Every single year. I'm joining their booth next year, since I knit now." Her chin lifts with pride.

Marianne has taken to knitting the same way I have taken to needlepoint.

This week has been filled with baking and needlepoint for me. Agnes was right; it did calm my nerves. Every time I would recall a particularly acerbic snippet of Melanie's vitriol, I would pick up my needlepoint and work on my sunset scene. I love the look of it. Once I stopped trying to force knitting to happen and gave in to what worked for me, the world of crafting split itself open for my perusal, which is a gift I never thought I would get.

Rip calls the gymnasium to attention as a man in a mascot costume meanders up to the stage.

Carlos holds back his laughter quite poorly, his hand going over his mouth. "I didn't realize they made giant balls of yarn costumes. Is that Dwight?"

Marianne and I nod in unison, because now that I've lived in Sweetwater Falls for half a year, I can confidently say that I know who is inside the giant ball of yarn. "Yep. He's always dressing up as something crazy to match the town event."

Carlos' arm winds around Marianne's trim waist. "I love it. I need to get me one of those to wear around the office."

I snort into my hot apple cider at the mental image of the strait-laced lawyer dancing around his law office in a giant yarn costume.

Rip welcomes us all to the Knit Your Heart Out auction event in time with Yarn Dwight ripping the black cloth off the display table behind the podium with a flourish.

My breath stills in my lungs as I take in the contents of the table. "What... Is that..."

Logan stands on his toes to get a better look, but then Delia whaps him in the back of his head with a rolled-up magazine. "Hey, tall guy. Some of us can't see over your giant head."

Logan slumps back down, but he leans his chin forward to get a better look. "I can't believe you don't know what's up there, Delia. Aren't you supposed to be the one in town who knows everything about everyone?"

While it's true that Delia is the town gossip, that might be exactly why she knows nothing about the secret project. The people working on it wouldn't have dared mention it to her for fear of word getting out.

"What is it?" Frank calls out from beside Delia.

Rip grins at being the center of our undivided attention. "What you have here are handknitted dolls in the likeness of one hundred individual residents living in Sweetwater Falls. Each doll has beaded eyes and a special secret note in its pocket for the winner of the item."

I gape at the detail of the first doll he holds up, which is the one made in Rip's own likeness. "Take a look at my doll —no doubt the handsomest one in the bunch."

Chortles rise above the gasps of awe that fill the gymnasium.

"Each doll will not be sold for less than forty dollars, so get your pocketbooks out and let's start the bidding on... on me!"

"Forty dollars for a doll?" I comment. "I know it's hand-made, but wow. That's steep. If those sell, the As the Page Turns Book Club is going to be set for many years, swimming in all the books they could possibly read in a lifetime."

Marianne quirks an eyebrow at me. "You know they don't spend all the money on books, right?"

I frown at the notion. "No. Isn't this to raise money for their book club? What else does a book club spend money on?"

Marianne grins wickedly. "They buy their books for the year, sure, but then they buy the school's textbooks for the year, too. Then whatever is left over they use to take a trip."

"A trip?" Appreciation shines through in my features. "That's pretty cool. Where did they go last year? Fancy dinner in Hamshire? An afternoon at Apple Blossom Bay to check out the coast?" I haven't been to the coast yet, but I hear Apple Blossom Bay is a lovely beach town, and that the cozy vibe is not unlike Sweetwater Falls.

Marianne and Logan chuckle at my modest suggestion. Logan shakes his head. "Ho, no. They raised enough money to buy their books for the year, the school's books, and they all went on a cruise together. It was a seven-day cruise last year. I hear they're aiming for a fourteen-day cruise this year."

Marianne nods. "Agnes said that's the goal. They're going all out."

I balk at the extravagance. "Are you serious? This event is to send the book club on a cruise?"

Marianne nods. "Every year, and we all love it."

I laugh loudly, so much that several people turn to stare at me.

The bidding begins, so the attention returns to Rip on the stage, holding his own doll.

"Forty dollars!" someone calls out without a lick of hesitation.

"Forty-five!"

"Fifty!"

I hear the sound of the sheriff bellow out a hearty, "Fifty-five!"

On and on the bidding goes. I cannot imagine anyone spending ninety-five dollars on a doll, but apparently that is the going rate for a doll of the Town Selectman.

The next one up is a kindergarten teacher in town. Her doll is a hot commodity, as well. It seems all the parents of her students want to buy the doll for their child, so the bidding goes well over a hundred dollars without a blink.

The auction is intense, but everyone is smiling and enjoying the frenzy of the shouted bids.

I love this game. I bid on Bill's doll when it comes up for auction because I can't not. It's the cutest thing. They even got his bushy eyebrows and permanent scowl spot on. I want to put Bill around my house in various spots so he can silently judge whatever is going on.

The bidding escalates quickly, and before I know it, I am throwing caution to the wind, spending far more on a doll than I would on groceries for myself for the week.

Logan laughs at me when I shout a hearty "Eighty dollars! I need that doll, Rip!"

The opposing bid raises once more, and finally the Bill doll is mine for a solid ninety dollars.

I regret spending that much money instantly, but the second the grumpy Bill doll is cradled in my hands, I deem the entire experience as worth every penny. "He's so cute! Oh, I love how mean he looks!"

Marianne coos at my doll as if we are twin children admiring our toy and all the joy it will bring to our playtime.

I laugh at the details, loving that the hair is even balding in the right spots.

I don't know why I feel pressure behind my eyes. Maybe the hysteria of the auction and the bidding did me in, breaking off a part of my adult self so I could reach that excitable child beneath.

"I don't know why I love this so much, but I do!" I can already picture Bill sitting on the kitchen counter, judging my meal because it isn't the horrid broccoli cheese soup that only he enjoys.

I hug my doll to my chest. "This is my favorite thing I've bought myself in a long time, and that's including the industrial mixer that I adore."

I hug my doll as the bidding goes on, jumping up and down when Marianne wins the doll of Agnes.

Our dolls talk to each other, fighting because that's

what they would do if Bill got out of line, which he always does.

A few minutes later, several more dolls have been auctioned off, but Marianne and I are still playing pretend.

Like cool adults should.

Carlos interrupts us with an excited, "Look! Marianne, it's you!"

Marianne lifts her head, gaping at the spectacle. "Are you serious? Why would they make a doll of me?" Her cheeks flame immediately. "Who would want that?"

Before Rip can call for the bidding to start on Marianne the Librarian, Carlos already has his hand up. "Forty dollars to the out-of-towner!"

Rip points to Carlos and then to the challenger—an elderly woman I've seen in the library before whom Marianne helps often.

Carlos will not be outbid. He doesn't hesitate to raise over and over until everyone else falls away.

It is the sweetest display of their relationship.

It is also something Jeremy would never have done for her.

Carlos brings back his Marianne doll gingerly, as if he is carrying a live baby. The dolls are all around ten inches tall, and absolutely perfect.

I coo at the details. "Oh my goodness! I love it so much. You've got a little book in your hand! That is the cutest thing!"

Marianne burrows her face in Carlos' shoulder. "You didn't have to buy that."

Carlos shrugs. "What? I've got a new office in serious need of some decorations."

Marianne chuckles into his shoulder. "I like that you're here."

He motions to the doll and hands it to her to hold and admire. "I like that you're here. And now I'll have you at my office with me all day long."

I love the two of them together.

I love them even more when Carlos lets Marianne and me add the Marianne doll to our moment of pretend, so Bill can get good and mad that they don't sell broccoli and cheese soup in the library.

I am so engrossed in my ridiculous play with my best friend that I don't understand why everyone suddenly turns to stare at me.

Logan elbows me in the side. "It's you! They made a doll of you!"

My mouth falls open as I gape at the perfect likeness of me, clothed in jeans and my lavender cardigan with an apron overtop. I am transfixed by the spitting image of myself—smiling with my curly blonde hair in a ponytail atop my head. I have a cupcake in my hand, which Rip tips to the doll's mouth so you can feed the Charlotte doll one of her own cupcakes.

"But I'm new in town," I argue, confused that I would be granted such a high honor.

Marianne bumps her hip to mine. "Actually, you're one of us. I think that doll proves it."

That thought washes over me in shades of wonder and appreciation. I was the new girl from the big city, but not anymore. Now I am their cupcake queen—a business owner in the small town I adore.

"It's the Halloween cupcake," I comment breathlessly, because of course the flavor of the cupcake is the thing I notice.

Rip confirms my suspicions. "For those of you lucky enough to have ordered the October Flavor of the Month from the Bravery Bakery, this one comes complete with a cricket on top, just like the real thing."

Carlos blanches, but I am enraptured at the details they captured. My words come out breathless. "It was a pumpkin spice latte cupcake with a cream cheese frosting, topped with an edible cricket."

Marianne squints as she leans forward. "Is that... They did! They put a knitted cricket on top of the cupcake!"

Laughter bubbles out of me. That was the month I promised a scream with each cupcake purchase.

I feel like I delivered on that one.

Apparently, the women in the As the Page Turns Book Club thought it was a memorable enough cupcake to warrant it being knitted onto my doll.

I cover my mouth with my hand as I hold my Bill doll to my chest. "It's me. I love it."

Logan raises his hand and calls out a confident "Forty dollars!"

Frank calls out from behind him, challenging the bid, but Delia scoffs at him, as if he has crossed some relationship line in bidding on another girl's doll.

Luckily, their tiff is short-lived because Logan tops it with an even fifty.

This entire event is surreal, so much that I have to find Aunt Winnie in the sea of faces to make sure I am not dreaming.

My great-aunt winks at me, letting me know that this is exactly the kind of fun I should be having, and the kind of life only the lucky get to live.

I am lucky, because I live here with these amazing people that I love.

I have only been in this town half a year, but I have made friends who know me well enough that I am recognizable to the town I love.

No one else challenges Logan's bid, no doubt because they know we are dating, and he is being precious to me.

Logan is always sweet to me, which isn't a gift I thought I would ever experience. I never chased after relationships or held them in any real esteem. But I love the time I get to spend with my police officer, even if a bulk of it is spent trying to solve crimes and muddle through murders together.

Logan collects his prize and shuffles back through the

crowd to my side, pulling me into a hug. "Look at her," he marvels.

I study with acute fascination the details of the doll as wonder stirs in my soul. "She looks happy."

Because I am in my hometown with the people I love, I actually am.

The End.

CARAMEL CORRUPTION CUPCAKE RECIPE
YIELD: 12 CUPCAKES

"It's an applesauce cinnamon cupcake. The peanut butter buttercream has a kick of cloves to cut the sweetness. Then I crushed pretzels and made caramel corn for the topping."

-Caramel Corruption, by Molly Maple

For the Cupcake:

1/2 cup unsalted butter at room temperature

1/2 cup granulated sugar

2 eggs at room temperature

1/2 tsp pure vanilla extract

1 cup unsweetened applesauce

2 cups all-purpose flour

2 tsp baking powder

½ tsp salt

½ Tbsp cinnamon

¼ tsp ground nutmeg

1/8 tsp ground cloves

Instructions for the Cupcake:

1. Preheat the oven to 350°F.
2. Using a stand mixer, cream ½ cup unsalted butter and ½ cup granulated sugar in a large mixing bowl.
3. Add eggs one at a time and beat until fluffy and light in color.
4. Add ½ tsp pure vanilla extract and 1 cup applesauce. Mix until well combined.
5. In a medium bowl, sift together 2 cups all-purpose flour, 2 tsp baking powder, ½ tsp salt, ½ Tbsp cinnamon, ¼ tsp nutmeg and 1/8 tsp cloves.
6. Slowly mix dry ingredients into applesauce mixture until just combined. Do not overmix.
7. Divide the batter into your 12-count lined cupcake pan, filling each one 2/3 the way full.
8. Bake for 15 minutes at 350°F, or until a toothpick inserted in the center comes out clean.
9. Let them cool in the pan for 10 minutes, then transfer to a cooling rack. Cool to room temperature before frosting.

Ingredients for the Peanut Butter Buttercream Frosting:

½ cup butter, softened

1 cup creamy peanut butter

2-3 Tbsp milk, as needed

2 cups confectioner's sugar

¼ tsp ground cloves

Instructions for the Peanut Butter Buttercream Frosting:

1. Cream ½ cup butter and 1 cup peanut butter in a stand mixer until well combined and light in color.
2. Add half the confectioner's sugar with ¼ tsp ground cloves, then 2 Tbsp milk. Mix until fluffy.
3. Add the other half of the confectioner's sugar, and an additional Tablespoon of milk as needed. Mix until fluffy.

*Top with crushed pretzels or caramel popcorn.

Enjoy a free preview of *Red Velvet Villainy*, book seven in the Cupcake Crimes series.

CHAPTER ONE

The Soup Alleyoop

*I*f an onlooker were to guess at which person would have more pep in their step on a crisp February morning, the safe bet would normally be on the twenty-eight-year-old, rather than the ninety-one-year-old woman. But today, my great-aunt Winifred outpaces me easily as she makes her way from my red sedan into the restaurant.

I'm not totally sure why this particular place stood out to Aunt Winnie as the perfect location for the Valentine's Day party she wants to throw. The Live Forever Club is always up to something fun—casino nights, skinny dipping, painting by moonlight... The three elderly women I adore are the shining stars of the cozy town of Sweetwater Falls. I wouldn't have thought the Soup Alleyoop would be on Aunt Winnie's radar of venues for a Valentine's Day Roaring Twenties-themed party, but I've learned my aunt is rarely wrong when it comes to showing the world how to have a great time.

I have only been in this restaurant once, being that I am still considered new in town. I have been proud to call Sweetwater Falls my home for over half a year now, but even that amount of time hasn't been enough to draw me back to a restaurant that is part basketball arcade games, part restaurant that only sells soup.

It's a niche market, I can say that.

The faux gymnasium honey-colored wood floors do not announce fine dining, though the place is clean enough. I recall the waitstaff wearing referee outfits with whistles dangling around their necks.

I look around at the red carpeted walls and the sports memorabilia in frames scattered about the place and wonder how much work this venue will take to jazz it up for the Live Forever Club's event.

Aunt Winnie presses the back of her hand to her cheek to warm it from the frigid snowy outdoors. "Yoo-hoo! Gus! Anybody here?" She cranes her neck after stomping the snow off her boots, but there is no one at the counter where you order your food.

I shrug. "Are we early?" I glance to the side to check the large neon scoreboard that tells the time. "Three minutes early. I'm sure they're just in back, firing up the soups. Why don't you walk me around and tell me what you want for your event? I've never been to a Valentine's Day event in Sweetwater Falls." I bat my lashes at her. "Is it all romantic and filled with pink paper hearts?"

Aunt Winnie chortles at my guess that I didn't think would be all that far off the mark. "Romance is for every day, if you want it. Valentine's Day around here is for intrigue. Fun. Mischief. Memories." She bats her hand at me. "Pink paper hearts aren't all that mischievous, so I pass on those."

I press my hand over my sternum and feign a gasp. "Mischief? You? I don't believe it."

Aunt Winnie takes her mittens off and stuffs them in the pockets of her winter coat. She loops her arm through mine and moves me toward the tables. "We want the theme to be the shadier side of the twenties. These booths are perfect. We can convert them into mini speak easies. Imagine everyone all dressed up in their best flapper wear, ordering fancy cocktails and whispering salacious secrets."

I smile at my Aunt's vision for the party. "That sounds fun."

"More than fun. Everyone is going to have a mission when they get here. A secret they have to solve."

"For example?"

Aunt Winnie's sea-green eyes dance with mischief. "You'll walk in and be handed a folded piece of paper. Maybe yours will say something like, 'Make sure the bartender puts three olives in your martini.' Then someone else will get a piece of paper that reads, 'Find the person who has three olives in their martini and ask them what sort of socks they think the mayor wears when he goes dancing.' Things like that. Finish your mission and come get another." She elbows me. "I was thinking of having some cute cigarette girls, only instead of handing out cigarettes, they'll hand out the secret missions."

I clap at her playful nature. "Conversation starters that work like a covert game. I love it!"

I know my best friend won't have a single issue with getting all dressed up with fancy twenties-style hairdos so we can play along with the Live Forever Club's hijinks.

I smile at my great-aunt, wondering how I got so lucky that I get to be the one with whom she shares her imagination. "And you think the Soup Alleyoop is the place for your party?"

Aunt Winnie motions around the sports-themed dining area. "I wouldn't mind having it here. It's a nice, open space in the center, which we'll need when the dancing starts. We'll bring in our own hors d'oeuvres and a bartender, so the menu isn't an issue."

Thank goodness. I love soup as much as the next girl, but it's not on my top list of things to eat on Valentine's Day.

Aunt Winifred hums to herself, motioning to the end of the room. "I'm bringing in a swing band. We're going to have a platform built over there, and dancing in the center area here."

Her hips begin to sway. Her eyes close because she is transporting herself either to the distant past or to the near future, where there will be a Valentine's Day party in which there will definitely be dancing.

Aunt Winifred keeps her eyes closed as she turns to me and scoops up my hand in a quickstep. I am uneducated in how to follow with any sort of prowess. Though, I waste no time trying to keep up. I wish I knew how to dance, but with my five-foot-ten inches and zero musical training, I was destined to move like the Tin Man in desperate need of an oil can.

Aunt Winnie doesn't mind my mechanical movements. What she would mind is me not moving at all—not trying to live a little, even if I manage the feat ungracefully.

I trip over my own two feet when she tries to twirl me, which is to be expected. I laugh without holding back, as is my way around any member of the Live Forever Club. "You're about to find out what a dreadful dancer I am."

"Nonsense." Aunt Winnie uses my hand to guide me in and out, her feet shuffling quicker and with more skill than I can muster in my clunky winter boots.

Clumsy as I am, I don't mind the levity one bit. "You need to give me lessons, or I'm going to embarrass myself on the dance floor at the party."

Aunt Winnie hums the melody that we dance to, ending our quickstep when she pulls me in and gives a big "da-da-ta" finish. Then she turns us and bows to our imaginary audience, batting her free hand at them. "Oh, go on. Stop your wild applause! What, you've never seen two heartbreakers dance the night away?"

I giggle through my bow. "Please tell me the dancing at your party will be just as lively. I've never received an imaginary standing ovation before, if you can believe it."

"I absolutely don't believe it. You're a natural on the dance floor." Aunt Winnie glances around the place to avoid my dubious look at her flagrant compliment. "You could be receiving a real standing ovation if the manager was here." Her smile falls. "Where is Gus?"

The front door opens, triggering the chime overhead, which is a recording of a roaring crowd. As silly as this restaurant is, I like the extra touches that make it truly unique.

I mean, if there were two Soup Alleyoops in the world, that would be an oddity I would need to see to believe.

The person walking into the restaurant is a guy who can't be older than sixteen, which seems to be the key demographic for this place. He carries a basketball under his arm and looks to be ready to put it to use.

He waves to us, nodding to Aunt Winifred. "Hey, Winnie. My mom is real excited for your Valentine's Day thing." He grins, showing off his braces. "My dad is mad at you because he doesn't want to get dressed up. He says people owned sweatpants back in the nineteen-twenties, so he should be able to wear them to the party, no problem." He snorts his amusement as he moseys his lanky form to the empty ordering station. "I think my mom is going to win that argument."

Aunt Winifred strolls over to him, taking me along with her when she loops her arm through mine. "She'd better. I've been known to turn away people who don't take parties seriously."

"Parties are a serious business?" I ask her.

Aunt Winifred nods without caveat. "Absolutely. There is nothing more important than fun." She tilts her head up at the high school student. "Greg, have you met my niece yet?"

"You're the new girl, right? The Cupcake Queen? That's what my little sister calls you."

If there is anything that can pull a grin to my face, it is that label. "Cupcake Queen? That is quite the honor. I'm Charlotte. And yes, I own the Bravery Bakery. Something tells me your little sister might just be one of my favorite people in Sweetwater Falls if that's what she calls me."

"Her birthday is next week, and my mom promised her she was going to place an order of cupcakes for her birthday party. But my sister is waiting for your flavor of the month to come out before she commits to which kinds she wants."

My hand flies to my heart. "What's your sister's favorite flavor?" I decide on the spot that I am going to open up a new facet of my business. "I might just throw in an extra special cupcake for her because it's her birthday."

Birthday cupcakes. That's a thing, right? It takes me a total of ten seconds to decide that yes, if you place a cupcake order for your birthday, then you get a bonus cupcake, which is a birthday cupcake. I can add a checkbox on the website so they can mark if the order is to celebrate a birthday.

Greg chatters away, grinning while he talks. "It's a big one, too. Double digits. Gracie is turning ten. And she likes anything with sprinkles. The more the better. Like, if you can see the frosting, it's not enough sprinkles."

A thrill lifts my posture so that I am bobbing on my toes. "That's wonderful! I'll make sure she gets her birthday cupcake. Extra sprinkles."

Greg cranes his neck to see if he can peek into the back, where there are smells of soup, but no bustling in the kitchen area to clue us in as to whether or not the staff is actually here. "I was hoping to get in a few rounds of free-throw practice before I have to start my homework, but I don't see anybody." He cups his hands over his mouth. "Hey, Gus! I'm about to start shooting hoops without ordering anything. I think you're going to give me that exasperated smile that means you're secretly frustrated but are too nice to say anything about it." Greg glances around when there is no response.

"Maybe he's not here yet." Aunt Winnie frowns at the empty counter. "But then why was the front door unlocked?"

Greg shrugs and then slaps Aunt Winifred's hand on

his way to the other side of the restaurant, where the free-throw hoop is set up. "I tried."

While I am content to try calling the restaurant to bring someone to the phone, Aunt Winnie has her own way of speeding things up.

She has no qualms going behind the desk where people place their orders, even as I shout-whisper to her that we aren't supposed to be behind the desk, because we are not employees.

Aunt Winnie waves off my worry. "Oh, pish-posh, honey cake. We tried following the rules. Now we're going to see what's cooking back here, so we can get to some serious party planning."

"Isn't that an oxymoron? Serious and parties?"

Aunt Winnie draws her short stature up, tossing her silver curls over her shoulder. "Darling, I am always serious about parties."

I love that she can say things like that with total confidence. Her war cry for me has been that I will become Charlotte the Brave, but it is only in spending time with her that I am learning how to find my voice and really put some volume to it.

I take a deep breath as if preparing to go underwater, then I steal behind the desk that is surely for employees only.

I feel like I am in grade school, doing something I know I should not and hoping the teacher doesn't find out. My stomach knots because I don't want to get in trouble, especially not by this Gus person, whom I don't know. If his first encounter with me is trespassing in his kitchen, I will for sure be a horrible person in his mind.

I hate breaking rules, yet it seems that if I am going to keep up with the Live Forever Club, one day, I'll need to get used to living on the wrong side of the law.

Or the wrong side of the counter, as it were.

As soon as I step where I shouldn't be, a foul smell hits my nose. I pride myself on being able to pick out notes of even the smallest flavor in a recipe, but this stench makes me wish my nose wasn't quite so perceptive.

"Ack. Scorched tomatoes and something rotting. Gross," I mumble to myself. Here's hoping that the menu for the big party smells better than this. If soup is the only thing on their menu, I certainly hope this isn't their prized product, because I cannot imagine anyone ordering seconds.

Aunt Winnie has no such qualms about the smell or her intrusion into the sacred space as she moseys through the narrow kitchen. "Gus? Oh, goodness."

I rush to her side when I see the problem. There is a pot of soup on the stove that has boiled over. My nose crinkles as I cast around for oven mitts. "That's going to be a pain to clean up." The tomato soup has splattered all over the industrial stove, giving the entire area a spattered red paint job.

Aunt Winnie turns off the burner while I locate two oven mitts so I can move the pot off the heat source.

I wince when the soup spits its burning lava onto the tender flesh of my wrist. "Oh! That stings."

Once I have the pot off the burner, I rush to the sink and run my wrist under a stream of icy water. I hiss through gritted teeth when the burn doesn't cool quick enough for my liking. While I've burned myself loads of times, the inside of my wrist has never toughened up.

Aunt Winnie winces. "Oo, that's going to leave a mark."

After I turn off the water, I cast around for something with which to dry off. My feet take me to the closet next to the back exit to search for a towel, and to clean up the tomato splatters on the surfaces and floor.

Aunt Winnie clucks her tongue, and I know she is thinking she can't believe the kitchen was left with a burner on. Aside from the food being ruined, it's a safety hazard I am grateful we were here to fix. "This isn't like Gus. He would never leave his kitchen messy. He's an orderly sort of man. Keeps a clean house. The business is always spotless." She frowns, looking around at the state of the stove and floor. "I don't understand."

I wipe down my kitchen every time I use it. Being without a space to create my own cupcake flavors for so long has made me extra appreciative of the industrial kitchen I now have.

But when I open the closet door, the mess of the kitchen is the last thing on my mind.

"Ah!" I shout incoherently. I don't mean to startle Aunt

Winnie, but I am not sure there is an elegant or tranquil response to announce what I am seeing.

Horror twists my pleasant expression as I take in the man on the floor, who is bound, gagged and limp against the mop and bucket. His legs are bent at uncomfortable angles, suggesting he was shoved into the closet after he was attacked.

Aunt Winnie is at my side, her mouth agape. "It's Gus! Quick, Charlotte, call Logan. Call a doctor, too!" She leans in as I take a step back. "Gus! Oh, dear. Is he..." Her voice catches at the possibility that her friend might be here only in body but not in spirit.

I fumble with my phone and place the quickest call I can manage because polite language escapes me. "Gus... Soup Alleyoop. Body in the closet. Logan, he's..."

But before I can announce that Gus is dead, Aunt Winnie leans in and presses two fingers to the side of Gus' awkwardly bent neck. "There's a pulse!"

My own heart rate races at the good news. Relief floods me, but it is quickly chased away by the angst of wondering who would possibly do this to an old man.

Logan is a fantastic boyfriend and a good cop, but even perfection has its limits. "Charlotte, what? Did something happen at the Soup Alleyoop? Are you okay?"

"Ambulance," I insist. "Ambulance for Gus." I can't hear Winifred's fretting nor Logan's worry. I can only hear the thrum of my heartbeat roaring in my ears. "Come quick, Logan. Gus has been attacked. He's alive now, but it doesn't look good."

My palms are sweaty even as Logan promises he's on his way, and he's bringing an ambulance on his heels. I hold the device to my sternum, my lips parted with equal measures of shock and dread. I cannot believe someone would hurt a man with sparse bits of white hair.

And if they came for Gus and hurt him so horribly, will they return to finish him off?

Read *Red Velvet Villainy* today!

ABOUT THE AUTHOR

Author Molly Maple believes in the magic of hot tea and the romance of rainy days.

She is a fan of all desserts, but cupcakes have a special place in her heart. Molly spends her days searching for fresh air, and her evenings reading in front of a fireplace.

Molly Maple is a pen name for USA Today bestselling fantasy author Mary E. Twomey, and contemporary romance author Tuesday Embers.

Visit her online at www.MollyMapleMysteries.com. Sign up for her newsletter to be alerted when her next new release is coming.

45283663R10114